D1082891

generations

generations

richard Matheson

GAUNTLET PRESS

■ 2012 ■

Generations
© 2012 by Richard Matheson

FIRST EDITION
10-digit ISBN: 1-934267-33-3
13-digit ISBN: 978-1-934267-33-2

Jacket Art © 2012 by Harry O. Morris and Bob Quinn
Interior Page Design by Dara Hoffman-Fox

Manufactured in the United States of America

Gauntlet Publications
5307 Arroyo Street
Colorado Springs, CO 80922
(719) 591-5566
www.gauntletpress.com
info@gauntletpress.com

LIMITED EDITION

With love to my first family

introduction

by richard matheson

When I first considered writing an introduction to my book—the word which occurred to me was *hybrid*. I immediately thought it inaccurate. I was thinking of the modern automobile which has two elements: the electric motor plus a gas engine. To be certain I checked the dictionary and ran across the phrase—the offspring of genetic parents. Nothing about two offspring. I took that as evidence that my book could be called a hybrid.

The book has three parts. The first part is a novel, in the traditional sense of a story with a beginning, a middle and an end. Third person prose; past tense. The second part of the book is the groundwork for a stage play, which I hope to see produced some day. That was how it started. Accordingly, I have labeled the book with stage terms, such as Overture, Act One and Act Two.

Part three, the third element, is biographical fantasy in that the events described never took place—though I believe they could have and should have. Such is the tragedy of my family.

Thus the generation of Generations.

—Richard Matheson
August 2011

generation gen·er·a·tion(jĕn'ə-rā'shən)

Noun
The term of years, roughly 30 among human beings, accepted as the average period between the birth of parents and the birth of their offspring.

Verb
The act or process of generating; origination, production, or procreation.

overture

The strangeness of this account is that it never happened. It could have happened. It might have happened. For that matter, it *should* have happened. If there was honesty and justice in the world, it certainly should have taken place as I described. Or close to it.

That's the thing, you see. Many fiction writer's have described incidents from their past, containing actual dialogue and/or declarations. That's where this account differs. The people described were real enough. What isn't real is what they say. That isn't exactly true either. What they say, they might well have said on a similar occasion. That occasion never occurred as far as I know. Accordingly, all the revelations remained unspoken. Is that clear? *This account never took place.* Maybe fragments of what is said were spoken here or elsewhere, at other times. Probably not though. That's' the point. One wishes that all these times had really taken place as described. To repeat: *They should have.*

~~~~~~~~~

My family is pure Norwegian. What I mean by that is that all family members, alive or not, immigrated from Norway or were born of Norwegian stock. Later generations were (and are) not pure Norwegian, of course. I hope they would understand this account and not take issue with it. The people described in my story are all pure Norwegian.

You will meet them one by one: my mother, brother, sisters, uncles, aunt and cousins. Pure Norwegian every one of them. Speaking words I never heard them speak but wish I had.

You have noticed, I'm sure, that I have not mentioned my father. He was pure Norwegian, too, but didn't take part that afternoon. He had been dead for ten years.

His funeral is imagined by me as having taken place in the early afternoon of my account. His date-altered demise is the genesis of the gathering that never happened. The event which never took place.

~~~~~~~~~~

The locale for my make-believe account is real enough. At least it was on that imagined afternoon in 1956. Not that 1956 is imaginary. It is what I say happened in 1956 that didn't happen. Confusing enough? How else can I express it? It all didn't happen to real people in a real house in a real year. Enough said. On with the story. I mean the account.

The house of the non-occurrence was on Bedford Avenue in Flatbush. It was one of two houses wedged between a brick office building and a Jewish Temple. I have memories of the Rabbi's singing, the side door of the temple open. On the other side, the office building had a candy store in its corner. I remember buying ice cream cones there. They were called, to my recollection, GOBS.

My Uncle Tollef and my Aunt Evelyn did janitorial cleaning in that building. One of the businesses must have been a travel agency, or something like it, because they gave my uncle a gazebo, which he rebuilt in his back yard. I recall many a summer evening meal enjoyed in that open gazebo.

I also recall the police raiding one of the offices full of slot machines and breaking them up with sledgehammers. My uncle took one of the slot machines home and repaired it. We played with it often.

The house was two stories tall with three bedrooms on the second floor, one bathroom. My cousin Francis had one bedroom, about the size of a closet. We spent many an hour having fun in that diminutive room.

His sister Vivian had one of the other two bedrooms. Uncle Tollef and Aunt Evelyn had the third.

There was also an attic. In it, Francis—we called him Franny—constructed a cabin airplane against a wall. It was an impressive accomplishment, with two seats, full dashboard, (taken from an old car) a steering wheel and a small glass windshield. I was not permitted to take the second seat. I was not that very companionable at that age. Francis kept me in abeyance by providing me with a single passenger motorboat which kept me on the opposite side of the attic. It had no motor but a crawl-in cabin and a miniscule stove made of plywood and two hooks for heat control. I wasn't crazy about it but had no recourse. I played my lone character in wordless silence.

It was one of many make-believe melodramas we absorbed ourselves in. There was also a complex plot populated by imaginary heroes who flew model airplanes. Franny's plane was taken from, I believe, a magazine called *Bill Barnes Air Trails*. His plane was, as I believe, called the Snorter. Maybe not. He built immaculate models of our flying forces. I think one of mine was Richtofen's tri-wing Fokker, which gives you an idea of my status. I remember for sure the name of Franny's imagined hero. It was Kent Grayson. He always won the contests. We had resumes of our "teams." Complete with faces scissored from a Sears Roebuck catalogue. There was a head mechanic called "Wing." Which team he was on I don't recall.

I do recall that Franny's co-pilot in his attic plane was a neighbor, George Mulroy. George was a pleasant, cooperative game player, unlike me, who was invariably temperamental. He never complained as I did.

Franny was the absolute game-player in charge. He was several years older than us. But it was more than that. He was a genuine leader. How this all played itself out is a big part of the unread tale told but never happened. Oh, enough. It didn't take place. But should have. Amen.

One more vivid memory. Francis owned a beautiful pistol, which he utilized in many of our imaginary dramas. One afternoon George and I showed up at Francis' house anticipating more entertaining dramaturgy. Instead, we found a note left by our leader. We were to look in the area built above the gazebo. There, to our shock, we found the beautiful pistol in fragments, a grim note from Francis with it. He was now too old to play games. Accordingly, he was destroying the pistol. George and I were stricken by the enormity of Franny's sacrifice. Game playing was over. George and I tried to reinstate it but, without Francis, it was no use.

~~~~~~~~~~

The main locale for this never-happened happening was on the ground floor of the Bedford Avenue house. Not entirely in the main room. There was a front hall, a step-down kitchen and a backyard; where the gazebo had been re-built. The account, except peripherally, did not occur in those parts of the house's ground floor.

Most of the story, which never took place, took place in the family room of the house. September of 1956. Not that I ever heard it referred to as the family room in those days. That's what that room was though. It was a room in which all family activities took place.

The room adjoined the parlor, which was always gloomily illuminated, even on a sunny day, because of the front porch roof.

On the other side of what I call the Family Room, was the step down doorway to the kitchen. There was a door to an oversize closet on the back wall. Placed near the door was an enormous round table. It had ten chairs around it, eight of them matching the table, two commandeered from the kitchen—on that particular day (that is—the day which never took place but should have) the table was covered with platters of food.

Across the room from the table was an aged recliner chair; its upholstery faded brown leather, a control button on top of its right wooden arm. A floor lamp stood beside the chair, a sun-bleached shade on it. The walls of the room were lined with a number (three) of glass-fronted cabinets in which "good" dishes were displayed.

Almost covering the huge, round table was a flowered tablecloth on which were arranged the serving platters, some pseudo-crystal, some ordinary china. On the dishes was a selection of edibles—Jewish rye-bread, seeded dinner rolls, crackers and cheese spread, ham and salami (called Cincinnati), sliced turkey, roast beef, mayonnaise, coffee cakes and vanilla cookies—post-funeral goodies.

The light in the room was dim, the afternoon overcast, a slight wind blowing.

act one

Evelyn Nelson came in from the kitchen, a large cake platter in her hands. She was fifty-one years old, plump and grey-haired, with a pleasant but not pretty face. She was wearing an un-fashionable, flower-print dress and new apron. She placed the cake platter on the table and fussed with the table edibles, getting them arranged "just right." As she fussed, she began to sing "Sweetheart" from the Nelson Eddy-Jeanette MacDonald film, her voice on key but ordinary.

She was nearing the end of the song when her daughter Vivian came in from the kitchen carrying a small dish on which a quarter pound of butter sat. Vivian was twenty-seven, not unpretty but overweight, with grey-streaked brunette hair. She wore an unattractive print dress and a long-sleeve sweater.

Her comment was dry. "Bravo, Jeanette," she said.

"Silly," her mother muttered, not amused. "Is that the crystal dish?"

"The fake crystal dish?" Vivian said.

Her mother's answer was slightly irked, "Crystal," she said.

Vivian slapped the dish on the table.

"Imitation crystal, you mean," she said, her lips tightening as she turned back to the kitchen.

She almost collided with her brother as he lest the kitchen carrying a large electric coffee urn. Francis was thirty-two years old; five-foot-eight inches tall, slender and brunette. He had grown a mustache to hide, as much as possible, a severely cleft palate.

His mother asked, "Is there enough coffee left, do you think?"

"I don't know, Mom," Francis answered moving toward the table, "Maybe if Uncle Sven and Uncle Bob are the only ones who drink it."

"You don't think Gladys or Aunt Mary will?" his mother asked.

With a deep sigh, Francis set the urn down on the table, "*Heavy,*" he said. He drew in a deep breath. "I don't know about Aunt Mary," he said, "Gladys usually drinks Postum like her mom."

An obese beagle came waddling in from the parlor. Evelyn winced. "Oh, dear," she said. She called out, "Sister!"

"*Now* what?" Vivian responded.

"Take Boots back to your room!" Evelyn told her.

"She *was* in my room!" Vivian called back irritably.

"Well, she's not there now!" Evelyn said. She leaned over the beagle to pat her head. "Sweetheart, you're not supposed to be in here," she said gently. Boots wagged her tail, quivering with pleasure.

"*Boots, you nasty creature,*" Vivian said as she came in carrying a bowl of apples, green grapes and bananas.

Evelyn made a pained sound. "She's not nasty," she said. "She just wanted to share in the party."

Vivian snickered, "The *party?*"

"You know what I mean," her mother said.

Vivian grabbed Boots by the collar and started dragging her across the linoleum floor. "C'mon, *sweetheart,*" she muttered.

"*Don't hurt her,*" Francis told her.

"*I'm-not-hurting-her,*" Vivian snapped back.

"Turn on the light, son," Evelyn told him, "It's getting dark in here."

Francis string-pulled on the fringe-shaded lamp above the table, then turned on the floor lamp beside the recliner chair. Evelyn moved to the table and removed the top of the coffee urn. She looked inside. "I guess there's enough," she said.

"Unless Uncle Bob has to sober up," Vivian said as she pulled Boots into the parlor; Boots claws scrapping on the floor.

"*Sister*," Evelyn scolded. "You know he isn't drinking anymore."

"And Uncle Sven has a bushy head of hair," Vivian said.

"Oh, stop it," her mother said. She continued fussing with the table. "It certainly was a lovely service." She changed the subject.

In the parlor, Vivian snickered again. "*Lovely*," she said.

"Well it was," Evelyn said. "Mr. Armbruster spoke very well."

"Yes, he did," Francis said.

In the front hall, Boots yelped. Francis called out his sister's name angrily. Evelyn moved to the parlor doorway. "*Don't hurt her*!" she called.

"I'm *not*!" Vivian called back angrily.

"Well, it sure sounds like you are!" Francis yelled.

"Oh, go to hell," Vivian told him.

"*Sister*!" cried her mother.

"Well, she won't come up," Vivian said.

"Well… be nice to her," her mother said. "She's our darling."

"Our *fat* darling," Vivian answered.

"Sister, *please*," her mother said.

Vivian's voice was barely audible now. "What are you going to do when she dies?" She asked, "Have her *stuffed*?"

"*Sister*," her mother pleaded.

"Keep her sitting at the table with a napkin around her neck?" Vivian's voice was fading now.

"*Oh, please*," her mother said.

Francis was scowling. "Why is Boots her dog anyway?" he asked. "She doesn't even like her. She treats her like you know what."

"I know," his mother said. "I'd let her have Paddy, but she doesn't like her either. And Snubs is yours."

"I'd never let her have Snubs," Francis said. "Not the way she treats Boots."

Evelyn sighed. "I know," she murmured.

Upstairs, Vivian slammed the door of her bedroom. "Boots is now confined," Francis said.

Evelyn managed a smile. "Poor Boots," she said.

Francis held up the coffee urn wire. "Mom, this isn't long enough," he said.

"That's why we only use the urn in the kitchen," his mother replied.

"Well, we can't do that today," Francis said.

"No, we can't," his mother agreed. "I wish we could. Isn't there an extension cord in the closet?"

"I think so," Francis said. "I'll check."

He went inside the closet and, several moments later, came out carrying the rolled up extension cord. "Here we go," he said.

"Oh, good," Evelyn nodded, smiling. "*Coffee*," she muttered distastefully.

Francis plugged in the coffee urn and it lit up. Most of the extension cord lay on the floor. "Is it all right to leave it like that?" Francis asked.

"We'll tell people not to walk there," his mother said.

"Okay," Francis shrugged.

The front doorbell rang.

"There they are," Evelyn said, fussing at her hair.

"Maybe it's Pop," Francis replied.

"In his own house?" she asked.

"In case he forgot his key," Francis said.

"I don't think so," his mother said. "But go look."

"Okay." Francis moved toward the parlor. As he did, the doorbell rang again. "I doubt it's your father," Evelyn said.

Francis went into the parlor, calling, "*Coming!*" Evelyn quickly checked the array of plates, cups, saucers and silverware on the table, then turned toward the parlor. At the front door she heard Francis greeting the arrivals. She heard muffled replies.

Her sister Fanny and niece Gladys came in, both wearing dark topcoats and hats and carrying purses. "*Hello!*" Evelyn greeted them. She hugged her sister, kissing her on the cheek. "*Fasa*," she said. "How are you dear?" Fanny's returned smile was a little stiff. "I'm fine," she said.

Evelyn smiled and gave Gladys a hug and kiss. "How are you, darling dear?" she asked.

"Fine," Gladys answered, politely.

Francis helped his aunt off with her coat while his mother helped Gladys.

Gladys was thirty-seven years old; five-foot-ten inches tall, darkly blonde and not as attractive as her two brothers. Her figure was voluptuous. Her mother was fifty-three, five-foot-four inches tall, an attractive woman despite being a little over-weight. She was wearing a pale pink blouse, a string of pearls at her neck.

"The service wasn't too painful for you, was it?" Her sister asked.

"No, not at all," Fanny answered.

"I thought Mr. Armbruster's talk was lovely," Evelyn said.

"Yes, it was," Fanny agreed.

"Did you tell him so afterward?" Evelyn asked.

"I didn't have the chance," her sister said. "There were too many people talking to him."

Evelyn nodded. "I know," she said. "I would have loved to talk to him too but I had to get home and get ready for the family."

"Of course," Fanny said. "We'll thank Mister Armbruster in church on Sunday."

"Good idea," her sister said.

They continued talking while Francis carried the topcoats, Fanny's hat and the two purses into the parlor. Returning, he asked Gladys if she wanted to take off her hat. As he asked, he averted his gaze from her breasts and stomach. Gladys was six months pregnant.

"No, I won't be able to stay that long," Gladys told him. "Bernie works the night shift today and he's baby-sitting the girls right now."

"Well, I *hope* you can stay." Francis checked his pocket watch. "It's not three o'clock yet."

Gladys smiled politely. "We'll see," she said.

"Okay," Francis said.

"Did Alicia call?" Fanny asked her sister.

"Not since Thursday," Evelyn grimaced. "She said she couldn't come to the service."

"Why not?" Fanny sounded suspicious.

"She said Ethel and Helen had to work and she doesn't drive," Evelyn answered.

"She could have been picked up," Fanny said. "Bob would have done it. Or Sven could have picked her up. He doesn't live that far away from her!"

Evelyn's tone became grave. "You think she just didn't want to come?" she asked.

Fanny winced. "Oh, I can't believe *that*." she said, "She *always* got along with Bert."

"Maybe too much," Evelyn was immediately sorry that she'd spoken so impulsively.

"What do you mean?" Fanny asked. She sounded even more suspicious now.

"Well…" Evelyn was embarrassed now. "I mean, well, you know how unhappy Alicia was with Johnny. His drinking ruined her life. When she married him, she was a real beauty. We all know that. We also know what happened to her—what she became," she hesitated. "How much she ate."

"So?" Fanny asked, not understanding.

"Well…" Evelyn hesitated. "You remember Buddy's funeral?"

"Yes," Fanny said, still not understanding what her sister was getting at.

"At the gathering after the service, I was talking to Alicia and she said—what were her words?—Fanny is the luckiest one of us, married to a man like Bert. *I didn't agree with her, of course.* I'm *very* happy with Tollef. But that's what she said."

"So you think that's why she didn't come to the service?" Fanny said.

"Well… *Fasa* " Evelyn sounded exasperated. "I think maybe she was saying that she wished she married Bert instead of Johnny."

"I doubt that," Fanny said. She chuckled grimly. "If she's only known," she said, "Bert wasn't much of an improvement over Johnny."

"Well, maybe *I'm* the lucky one after all," Evelyn said, pleased. "Maybe that wasn't the reason Alicia didn't come today. Maybe she knew it was going to be an open casket and didn't like that idea."

"Oh, I don't know about that either," Fanny said. "Buddy's service was open casket too and that didn't bother her. And Buddy was her pride and joy."

"I know," Evelyn nodded. "Didn't Alicia ask Richard if he didn't want to kiss Buddy good-bye? Buddy was always nice to Richard."

"Yes, he was," Fanny said. "Richard didn't want to do it, though. It frightened him. I pulled him away."

"That's too bad," Evelyn said, sighing. "Well, I guess we'll never know why Alicia didn't come."

She turned away abruptly. "*Gladys,*" she said, giving her niece a big smile. She patted Gladys on the stomach. "Boy or girl?" she asked.

"Bernie would like another son," Gladys told her. "I'd prefer a girl."

Evelyn's smile was enraptured. "A lovely little girl," she murmured. "A gift from God." She gestured toward the table. "Well, sit, sit, everybody." She said.

Gladys and her mother sat down. Francis took a chair across from Gladys, one chair away from his mother, who sat down last.

"You're still wearing your hat," Evelyn said to her niece. Gladys explained to her about Bernie's nightshift

"Well, what a shame," Evelyn scolded lightly. "We hoped you could stay."

"Well…" Gladys didn't quite smile.

"Is that why Bernie couldn't make it to the service?" Evelyn asked.

Gladys' voice grew resistant as she answered, "He's baby-sitting the girls."

"*Oh,*" Evelyn looked disappointed. "You couldn't find a sitter," she said.

"*No,* we *couldn't,*" Gladys responded.

"And Doris isn't old enough to—?"

Gladys broke in, "*No,* Tante," she said. "She isn't.

"What a shame," Evelyn said. "We'd have loved to see the girls. And Philip, of course."

Francis spoke abruptly. "Have some food if you're hungry," he said. "A sandwich. A cookie. A slice of cake." Fanny smiled at him.

"You want Postum like Mama?" Evelyn asked her niece.

"No, I think I'll have a cup of coffee," Gladys said. "I didn't sleep that much last night."

"You're drinking coffee?" asked her mother. It was not a question.

"Yes. I am having coffee, Mom." Gladys answered. It was not an answered question.

"Is coffee okay for the baby?" Evelyn said.

"*Yes*," Gladys told her. "Just a cup."

"All right," Evelyn said. She turned to Francis. "Darling, would you bring Tante Fanny some hot water and the jar of Postum?"

"Okay," Francis said. Standing, he headed for the kitchen.

"Tante?" Gladys looked at the coffee urn.

Evelyn hesitated, then poured a half-cup of coffee.

"A *full cup*?" Gladys said.

"Yes, dear," Evelyn filled the cup and handed it to her niece. "Sorry, Fasa," she murmured. Fanny's smile was slightly pained.

"I was just telling your mother—" Evelyn started. Gladys interrupted.

"Isn't Vivian here?" she asked.

"She's up in her room," Evelyn said. "Boots got down by accident—"

Gladys said, "Boots?"

"Her dog. I told Viv to bring her back upstairs."

"Is she coming back down?" Gladys asked.

"Who, Boots?"

Gladys suppressed a smile. "Vivian," she said.

"Oh, she'll be down," Evelyn told her, smiling. "I thought you meant her dog."

"I'm sorry, I interrupted you before," Gladys said. "You said you were telling Mom something."

"I was?" said Evelyn. She thought about it for a moment, then said, "Oh, yes. Something about the service."

"What about it?" Gladys asked.

"Well, I thought it was lovely," Evelyn told her.

"It was nice," Gladys partially agreed.

"Your mother thinks that maybe Tante Lise didn't show up because it was open casket."

"*I didn't say that!*" Fanny protested.

"Well—" Evelyn made a shrugging motion. "Something kept her away."

"I doubt if it was the open casket," Fanny said. "Not that I liked it very much."

"I didn't like it at all," Gladys said. "Pop in that light brown suit I'd never seen him wear. His hair dyed black. His cheeks rouged. Lying there like an overstuffed doll. I hated it."

"So did I," her mother agreed.

Evelyn looked pained. "I thought he looked handsome," she said.

Fanny's lips tightened. "*Handsome?*"

"Well, I thought so," Evelyn said faintly.

Francis came back with a steaming pot of water and a jar of Postum. He handed the jar to his Aunt.

"Thank you, Francis," she said. He nodded. "You're welcome, Tante." He responded.

They all watched Fanny unscrew the top of the jar then, picking up a teaspoon, ladling a spoonful of Postum into the cup. Francis poured hot water into the cup and Fanny stirred its contents. "You sure you don't want any?" she asked her daughter.

"The coffee's fine," Gladys told her. She looked at Francis. "What did you think of the open casket?"

"Well—" Francis hesitated. Then he said, "It didn't really look like Uncle Bert."

"No, it didn't," Gladys said. "Not at all."

"You better put the kettle back in the kitchen, Francis," his mother told him.

He looked at her for several moments, then said, "Okay," and turned back to the kitchen. Evelyn drew in a deep breath. "Well, it *was* a lovely service," she said.

"Yes, it was," her sister agreed. "Open casket or not."

"Too bad he didn't look at all the way he did in the hospital," Gladys said.

"I'm sorry it bothered you," Evelyn said. "Every funeral I ever went to was open casket."

Francis re-entered the room. "Maybe they always have open casket unless you ask them not to," he said.

"You *know* this?" Evelyn asked in a dubious voice.

"Well…" Francis had no reply.

"Don't give opinions unless you're sure of them," his mother said. "*Where are you going?*"

Francis turned from the parlor doorway. "I thought I'd see if Snubs is all right."

"She's *fine!*" his mother said. "Stay here," she managed a smile. "Visit with our guests."

No one spoke while Francis sat down. His mother was sniffling now, apparently on the verge of tears.

"I'm sorry if it was painful," she said. "I didn't know."

"It wasn't that bad," Fanny told her. "Just a little unpleasant."

"I know," Evelyn took out a handkerchief and dabbed at her eyes.

"Don't be upset now," her sister said.

The doorbell rang and Francis stood quickly. "I'll get it," he said.

"Thank you, dear," his mother's voice was slightly broken. Fanny reached over to pat her sister's hand and they exchanged a thin smile. "Thank you, Fasa," Evelyn murmured. She drew in a ragged breath. "Have a danish," she said. "They're fresh. Tollef just bought them this morning."

"Maybe a small piece," Fanny gestured weakly as her sister put a large chocolate danish on a plate and held it out. "Just a piece," she said. "Maybe half a cheese."

"The chocolate's are awfully good," Evelyn said.

"I know," Fanny said. "Just half a cheese is plenty though. I have to watch my girlish figure."

"Oh, all right," Evelyn said. "Girlish figure, poo. How about you, Gladys? Can I talk you into a chocolate danish?"

"I'll just have a cookie," Gladys said.

Evelyn clucked disparagingly. "No one seems to want a chocolate danish," she said, looking sad. She handed Gladys two large cookies. "Just one," Gladys said. Evelyn made a sigh of rejection.

In the front hall, Francis had opened the door. He smiled broadly. "Uncle!" he cried.

"Nephew!" his uncle cried back. "It must be you!"

"It *is!*" said Francis, grinning.

"Our darling brother," Evelyn said. She handed Fanny more than half a slice of the cheese danish. "Too much, Evelina," her sister said. "Just eat what you want," Evelyn said, feigning deep injury. Fanny shook her head, smiling.

"You wanna leave your hat and coat in here, Uncle Sven?" Francis said in the parlor.

"*Sound* idea, nephew Francis," his uncle said.

In a few moments, Sven came into the family room. He was fifty-nine-years-old, five-foot-ten-inches tall, stocky and bald with grey hair over each ear. He wore a dark blue suit, a white shirt and patterned tie, sweater vest. His face was lightly florid.

"Afternoon, all," he said.

"Brother dear," Evelyn moved across the room to give him a hug and a cheek kiss.

"Evelina, my beloved sister," Sven said.

Evelyn snorted softly. "You're looking well," she said.

"I *am* well, Evelina," Sven responded. "A little better than Bert, anyway."

"*Sven*," she chided.

Sven turned toward Fanny, leaned over and kissed her on the cheek. "Beautiful sister, Fanny," he said.

"How *are* you, Sven?" she asked.

"Fair to middling, Fanny," he answered. "Sorry about Bert."

"We all are," she said. Her tone was flat.

"Well, not everyone," Sven said. "A few bartenders probably wish he was still around."

"I'm sure," she murmured.

"Bad joke, Fanny. Sorry." Sven apologized. He leaned over Gladys and kissed her cheek. She smiled. "Uncle."

"I hear you're with child," he said. She smiled. Again. "Boy or girl? Or both?" Sven asked.

"A girl, I hope," she answered.

"Well, it's one or the other," Sven said. "Family all well?" he asked. She nodded, smiling again. "How's Lily?" she asked.

Sven sighed. "Probably okay," he said.

"You don't know?" Gladys probed.

"Well… she was the last time I spoke to her," he told her.

"She couldn't make it today?" Gladys asked.

"No," he said. He straightened up. "*So*, are we all here?"

"Except for Bob and Mary. And Richard, of course," Evelyn said.

"Richard flew here from Los Angeles?" Sven sounded impressed.

"Well… Bert *was* his father," Evelyn said.

"*Was he really?*" Sven said, pretending genuine curiosity.

"*Sven*," his sister scolded.

"No, really," Sven said. "I just never saw them together." Sighing once more, he looked around. "No Alicia? Helen? Ethel?"

"Ethel and Helen are working," Evelyn told him.

"I had a job today," Sven said. "I cancelled it."

"I know," Evelyn nodded. "They might have come."

"Did Alicia ask you to pick her up?" Fanny asked.

"*Pick her up?*" Sven feigned astonishment. "I'd need a derrick."

Francis snickered and his mother looked at him disapprovingly.

Fanny repressed a smile. "You know what I mean," she said to her brother.

"You mean did she ask me to give her a ride," Sven said. "No, she didn't ask." He made a face. "I'm not sure my little Buick could have handled the extra weight anyway."

"Sven," Evelyn sounded critical but amused.

"That's me," said Sven.

"You're being cruel," his sister said.

"*Who? Me?*" said Sven. He sounded aghast. "I only speak the truth. Two-ton Alicia."

"*Uncle!*" "*Brother!*" Gladys and Evelyn cried out simultaneously. Francis burst into laughter and his mother frowned at him, trying to suppress her own amusement.

"Flung back to Earth by sister and niece," Sven said.

Everyone laughed. Then Fanny said, "We're being mean to Alicia."

"Alicia was mean to us," Sven replied.

"*When?*" Fanny asked.

"In Oslo, when we were kids," Sven answered.

"Oh, you're making that up," Fanny scolded.

"Coffee, Uncle Sven?" Francis asked as Sven took a seat next to Gladys. "I'll sit down then, control myself." Sven said.

"I doubt it," Evelyn said.

"Oh!" Sven cried in mock offense. "That from my own sister! Who I carefully raised from infancy!"

"Albert did," said Evelyn. "Have a sandwich."

"Have a sandwich," Sven repeated.

"*Coffee*, Uncle?" Francis asked. Again.

"Are you kidding?" Sven looked at his nephew in mock startlement. "In this den of Postum?"

Fanny laughed. "You could do worse," she said.

"I know, I know," Sven responded. "Mrs. Eddy said: Drink coffee and you go to blazes. Drink Postum – "

"Now you *know* she never said that," Fanny interrupted him. Sven gestured to Francis who filled a cup of coffee from the urn. "Sugar? Cream?" he asked.

"If I'm going to Hell, I might as well drink it straight," Sven told his nephew.

"Just stop it," Evelyn said.

"Yes, ma'am," Sven said. He took a sip of coffee.

"*Ah*," he said. "Uno sippo closer to Hell." Francis chuckled, pretending not to notice his mother's disparaging glance.

"You make too much of Postum," Fanny told her brother. "If none were available, I've been known to have a cup of coffee."

"*Fanny!*" Both Evelyn and Sven spoke her name in shock, Sven's make believe. "See you in the fiery pit," he said.

"It's a date," Fanny said with a little smile.

"You two," Evelyn scoffed. She held out a platter to Sven. "Ham? Turkey? Cincinnati?"

"No Chicago?" Sven said. He looked suddenly awed. "Aha!" he said. "Do I catch sight of Evelina Nelson's world-famous lemon cake?"

"You do," Evelyn said, pleased and smiling.

"Well, then, that's for me," Sven said. "A big slice of Evelina Nelson's world-famous lemon cake. *And* a cup of Evelina Nelson's world-famous coffee. *Perfect!*" Francis kept grinning as he added coffee to his cup.

Shaking her head, Evelyn started to slice the cake.

"Don't be cheap now," Sven insisted.

Evelyn made a disgusted sound and cut the cake slice twice as big. "Is that all?" he said.

"You want the whole cake?" Evelyn asked.

"Maybe," Sven answered, his tone sly. He took the plate of cake from his sister. "That'll do for now," he said.

"*Piggy*," Evelyn said.

"Oink," Sven replied. Then he said to Fanny, "Thank you for your coffee confession."

"It wasn't a *confession*," Fanny said, half serious.

"Well, sure it was," Sven insisted. "How abut you, Gladys? Are you a secret coffee drinker, too?"

Gladys only smiled and shook her head.

"*Come on!*" Sven said. "Tell us the low down! Do you sneak an illicit cup of coffee now and again?"

"Guilty," Gladys said, holding up her cup of coffee, trying not to smile.

"Ah-ha!" Sven cried. "Now we're getting somewhere! Anyone else? How about you, young man?" he addressed Francis. "Are you a coffee drinker on the sly?"

"A whiskey drinker," Francis said.

"*That's not funny*," Evelyn broke in angrily.

"*Oh…*" Francis scowled. "I'm just kidding, Mom."

"Well, it isn't very funny," his mother said. "Not at all."

"I'm *sorry*," Francis said. He didn't sound it.

"Thus concludes the family confession hour," Sven announced. "Tune in tomorrow when the topic will be—"

"Family Confession Hour, Part Two," Francis said.

Everyone stared at him. It hadn't sounded as though he'd been joking. "You *are* joking, aren't you?" asked his uncle.

"Well…" Francis hesitated, then declared, "Of *course* I am."

"I should hope so," Evelyn said. She turned to her brother. "I thought you used cream and sugar," she said almost accusingly."

"I do," Sven admitted. "Copious amounts."

Evelyn shoved the cream pitcher and sugar bowl across the tablecloth. "*There*," she said. She still sounded irritated.

"What a sloppy hostess," Sven said. He put cream and sugar into his cup and stirred them. "Got some brandy for this, sis?" he asked.

"If you don't stop—" Evelyn started.

In the front hall, the doorbell rang. "Saved by the bell," Sven said. Francis stood without a word and moved into the parlor.

"That must be Bob and Mary," Fanny said.

"Or the whiskey salesman," Sven suggested.

"*Sven*," Evelyn's tone was sharp.

"Maybe it's Alicia," Sven said, trying to keep a straight face. "No, she wouldn't ring the bell, she'd bash the door in with her rear end."

"I'm warning you," Evelyn said. The upturned corner of her lips belied her words.

"Sven, don't," Fanny pleaded.

"Done, sister dear," Sven answered.

In the front hall, they heard Francis open the door and greet Bob, Mary and Richard. "Richard came all the way from California?" Sven asked.

"He did," Fanny said.

"And *your* sister, Alicia, couldn't travel half a mile to be here?"

"That's right," Evelyn said.

"Let's not start that again," Fanny told her.

"Well…" Evelyn's lips tightened.

"He's married now, isn't he?" Sven asked. Fanny smiled. "With two children," she told him

"*Ooh*," Sven grimaced. "I'll never be the family historian. When did all this happen?"

"In the past four years," Fanny said.

"Yikes," Sven said. "Boys? Girls?"

"One of each," Fanny said. "A son—Richard."

"Why do fathers *do* that?" Sven sounded critical now.

"It was his wife's idea," Fanny said.

Sven nodded, "And the girl?"

"Alison," Fanny said. "Alison Marie."

"Good name," Sven said.

In the parlor, they heard Francis helping Bob, Mary and Richard take off their topcoats.

"I don't have a hat, Franny," Richard said.

"You can't come in then," Francis told him, sounding serious.

The three laughed. Coming into the family room, Mary first, followed by Bob, Richard and Francis.

Bob was forty-one years old, five-foot-eleven inches tall, slightly overweight, with thinning grey-brown hair. Not as handsome as his younger brother, he was still a good-looking man. He wore a black, pin-stripe suit, striped shirt and patterned tie. The last held in place be a gold clasp pin. Except for his red-tinted features, he was the image of a successful business executive.

His wife, Mary, was forty-years old, a once lovely Irish colleen. She was five-foot-six-inches tall, slender to the point of thinness, her hair an amalgam of brunette and grey. She wore a plain black dress and had a string of pearls at her neck.

Richard was twenty-eight-years old, six-foot-two-inches tall, well built, blonde and quite good looking. He was wearing dark brown slacks, a light blue shirt and black knit tie, a dark blue sport jacket with military buttons, black socks and loafers.

After coming in, Richard talked with Francis. Bob went immediately to his mother; she hadn't gotten up. Leaning over, he kissed her on the cheek. "Hi, Mom," he said. She squeezed his hand. "Hello, dear," she said.

"You look lovely, sweetheart," Bob told her. She smiled, patting his hand.

"I haven't seen you lately," she said.

"I've been so swamped, Mom," he explained.

"I miss you," she said.

"I know. I'm sorry," he apologized. "We'll go out to dinner some night next week."

Her answer was grave. "Don't do it if you're too busy," she said.

Mary, nearby, directed a gaze toward heaven.

Bob turned to Gladys, who was still sitting when her brother greeted her, bending over to kiss her cheek, she returned his greeting, politely, but subdued. "How's the baby?" he asked. "Growing," she said. Bob chuckled. "She'll probably be a big one," he said.

"Why? Because *I'm* so big?" Gladys said tightly.

"Not at all," Bob said cheerily. He looked down at her chest. "I'll tell you one thing, though," he said. "She'll never go hungry."

Gladys smile was close to arctic. "Just kidding," he said.

He turned to Evelyn. "*Tante*," he said. She gave him a hug and a cheek kiss. "I'm so glad you came."

"Wouldn't miss it, Tante," he said. Bob turned to Sven. "*Uncle*," he said, smiling.

"Nephew number two," Sven said. "Or is it number three?"

"Anything but number two, Uncle," Bob said.

Sven laughed. "That *was* a crappy thing to say," he said. They exchanged a chuckle.

Mary greeted Sven with a hug. "Uncle-in Law," she said.

"Oh, please," he said. "Not in-law."

"Sorry," Mary smiled at him warmly.

"Family all well?" Sven asked her.

"All well," she said. She returned Evelyn's hug and kiss. "Tante," she said.

"Hello, dear," Evelyn said. "Thank you for coming." Mary smiled again.

"You have—what?—ten—eleven daughters?" Sven asked.

Mary repressed a smile. "*Six*, Uncle," she said.

"No boys," Sven said.

"Not *yet*," Mary shook her head.

"You're planning on more?" Sven said.

"God willing," Mary answered.

"Well, if you do decide," Sven said. "I had two boys out of three tries. I must have some kind of secret."

"We had one of each," Evelyn broke in.

"*Which was more than enough*," Sven said. Evelyn looked at him curiously but said nothing.

"You look nice," Sven said to Mary. "That's a good-looking dress. Very…funereal?"

"I had no choice," Mary said.

"I didn't exactly wear a summer ensemble either," Sven replied. "Why do we do it anyway? Seems as though funerals could use a little pepping up. All that blackness. Fanny was right wearing pink."

"Death is black, I suppose," Mary said.

"And life is white," Sven said, nodding. "Unless you happen to be Marien Anderson."

Mary's smile faltered. "Who?"

"You know," Sven answered. "The negro singer."

"Oh," Mary nodded uncertainly.

"Care for some Postum?" Sven changed the subject. "There *is* coffee but you don't dare drink it. Not here."

"Now *stop* that," Evelyn scolded. "Pay no attention to him, Mary. He's just being silly."

Sven pressed his right index finger against his temple. "Good-bye cruel world," he said. He glanced at Evelyn. "Are Christian Scientists allowed to—you know—kill themselves?" he asked in an innocent tone.

"Uh!" Evelyn uttered a grunt of surrendering disgust and turned away, waving a dismissive hand at her brother. "They have such short tempers," Sven said. Mary snorted softly.

"You're not a Christian Scientist, are you?" Sven asked.

"Catholic," Mary said.

"Bob too?"

"No, just the rest of us," Mary said. "Lily here?" She asked, changing the subject.

Sven's voice became a little stiff. "She couldn't make it," he said.

"She all right?" Mary asked.

Sven shrugged. "I assume so," he said. He turned away.

During their exchange, Richard had leaned over his mother to kiss her on the cheek. "Hi, Mom," he said.

"You finally got around to your mama," she said.

"Now, Mom," he chided. "I was saying hello to Tante and Franny."

She smiled as though she didn't really believe it. "Of course," she said. She squeezed his hand. "How's my baby?" she asked.

"Your almost thirty-year-old baby," Richard said.

"*You're not thirty,*" his mother protested.

"Almost," he said. "In two years, no less. My birthday's in February."

"February twentieth, nineteen twenty-six, six P.M." Fanny said.

"Good Lord," Richard grinned. "You know what I weighed as well?"

"Seven pounds, six ounces," Fanny told him.

Richard chuckled. "Incredible," he said. Then, "How am I? Fine. How are *you?*"

Fanny sighed. "As well as can be expected," she said.

He smiled sympathetically. "I know. I'm sure it wasn't easy for you." His expression tensed. "At least it would have been if the casket was closed."

"At least," Fanny agreed.

"I'm surprised Tante Evelyn didn't ask me if I wanted to kiss Pop good-bye. The way Tante Lise did at Buddy's funeral."

"I wouldn't have let you," his mother responded firmly.

"I know," Richard said with a smile.

"How's Ruth?" his mother asked.

"She's fine," Richard answered.

"She couldn't come?" Fanny asked.

"No, the kids are too young to leave with a sitter," he told her. "We don't have one anyway."

"Oh, too bad," Fanny said. "Some other time."

"I better say hello to uncle Sven," Richard told her.

"Sit with me then," she said. She made a disappointed sound, glancing to her right. Francis had just taken the chair next to her. Gladys was on her left.

"I'll sit with you later," Richard said.

"I *hope* so," she said. Her smile was pained. Mary, nearby, directed another glance at the sky.

Richard forced a smile and turned to his uncle who had just spoken to Mary. She, who was, now, leaning on her mother-in-law to say hello.

"*Uncle Sven,*" Richard said, smiling.

"*Nephew Richard,*" Sven responded cheerfully.

They shook hands. "How are you?" Richard asked.

"Not too bad for an old Norwegian," Sven told him. "And you?"

"Okay."

"And the family?" Sven asked.

"Good," Richard replied.

"Sorry about your dad," Sven said.

"So am I," Richard replied. "I did hardly know him, though."

"I know that," Sven told him gravely.

Richard looked around. "Lily not here?" he asked.

"She couldn't make it," Sven said. Once more, his tone stiffened.

"She's not sick, is she?" Richard asked.

"No," Sven said. His reply indicated: *End of Conversation.*

"Hi, Mom," Mary said.

Fanny's response was polite. "Mary," she said.

"Feeling all right?" Mary asked.

Fanny sighed. "I'm fine," she said. She forced a smile.

"Good," Mary said. There, that's done, her manner seemed to say. She sat in the chair next to Gladys. "Hi," she said. Gladys nodded. "Hi," she replied. She didn't look at Mary.

"*Everybody sit,*" Evelyn said. It was in the nature of a command. Pleasant but commanding. Bob took a seat next to his sister; Mary took the chair to his left. "Sit here, Dick," Francis invited.

"I will," Richard said. "I just want to say hello to my sister."

He leaned over to kiss Gladys on the cheek. "Hello, Mother," he said.

"Hello, dear," she said. She gave him an air kiss.

"Due soon?" he asked.

"Three months," she said, smiling.

"Keep in touch," he said, smiling back at her. He looked at her breasts.

Evelyn said, "Richard. *Sit.*"

"Yes, ma'am." Richard sat on the kitchen chair next to Francis.

"If you're hungry, there's bread and cold cuts. *And* rolls. And cake and – "

"Evelyn Nelson's world-famous lemon cake," Sven interrupted. Richard laughed as Evelyn picked up a roll and poised herself as though to throw it at her brother. Sven threw up his hands in surrender. "*Kamerad*," he said.

"You'd better give up," Evelyn said. She looked back at Richard. "Cake and cookies and cole slaw and potato salad," she invited.

"And lions and tigers and bears; oh, my," Sven said.

"I give up," Evelyn said.

"A regular feast," Richard said to his aunt.

"Mom, shouldn't Vivian be down here?" Francis asked.

Evelyn looked at him questioningly. After a few moments she walked to the parlor doorway and called Vivian's name. There was no answer. "Vivian!" her mother shouted. Upstairs, there was a muffled response. "*Come down, sister!*" Evelyn cried. She looked distressed as she moved back to the chair next to the wall. "She'll be down," she said grimly.

"Dick?" said Gladys.

"Mother?" he responded.

"*Mother?*" Fanny questioned.

"Well, she's going to be," Richard said.

"And already is," Francis added.

"Oh," Fanny said. She didn't sound approving.

"What is it, Glad?" Richard asked.

"Why didn't you ask us to pick you up?" she said. "Bernie could have done it. You could have stayed at our house."

"Well…" Richard looked embarrassed. "I was talking to Bob on the phone—about Pop—and when I said I was wondering whether I should go to the funeral or not, he said I should and he'd pick me up at the airport. And I—" he faltered. "I could stay at his house."

"*Our* house," Mary contradicted.

"Yes," Richard said, nodding.

"We *do* have room at our house," Gladys said. "There's a couch in the living room that opens up into a bed. A double bed."

"We have the extra bedroom," Mary said. She tried to sound amiable but failed.

"I see," Gladys said.

"Glad, I didn't know you wanted Dick to stay at your house," Bob said. "You should have told me."

"I didn't *know* he was coming until today," Gladys said.

"Well—" Bob shrugged. "Another family brouhaha."

"No, no," Fanny declared. She would not accept it.

"Well, anyway…" Gladys said; her cool approach to making peace.

Silence. Then Bob said, "Tante Evelyn?" Evelyn looked at him. "I've been meaning to ask you for some time," he continued. "Where did you get this wonderful table? We need one just like it in our dining room."

"Maybe a trifle smaller," Mary said. Everyone laughed except Gladys. "No, just as big," Bob said. All but Gladys laughed again.

"I perceive a declaration of war," Sven said. More laughter and chuckling. Gladys smiled. "Well, maybe a little smaller," Bob said. More laughter. "Hubby concedes once more," Sven said. "Rarely," Mary told him. More laughter.

"Where did you buy it, Tante?" Bob asked.

"At a used furniture store that was going out of business," she said.

"Near the high school," Francis added.

"On the next block," Evelyn corrected.

"Do you mind me asking what you paid for it?" Bob asked.

"Oh, I don't know," Evelyn sounded uncomfortable. "Four or five hundred dollars, I guess."

"Two hundred and twenty dollars," Francis said. His mother gave him a cold look.

"*No*," Bob was incredulous. "I'd have paid a thousand."

"*You would*," Gladys muttered. "*Sold American!*" Francis said at the same time. Everyone laughed. "Thank you, bro," Mary said to Francis. The laughter increased.

"I hope that store is still in business," Bob said.

"It's not," Evelyn told him.

"Thank God!" Mary said. Everyone laughed again.

"Too bad," Bob said.

"Not for me," Mary said. More laughter.

"You see what I live with?" Bob said. "I'm just trying to prettify our house."

"Surrender, nephew," Sven advised. "It's the only way."

In the midst of the following laughter, Vivian came into the room, a surly expression on her face.

"*There she is*," Sven sang. "*Miss America*."

Bob turned to greet her. "Hello, Vivian."

"Hello," she said, her voice barely audible.

"Sit over here, sister," Evelyn said, gesturing toward the chair to her left. Vivian hesitated; then sat down. Everyone said hello to her and she mumbled back.

Now they were all seated, around the immense, round dining table. The cast of this improbable-desirable play. Which would never be performed but might have been, should have been. Not the entire cast, yet, Tollef Nelson wasn't home.

Evelyn sat in the chair next to the wall. To her right was Mary, to her left Vivian. Next to Mary was Bob, next to him, Gladys. To Gladys' right was Fanny, to Fanny's right, Francis. Richard sat between Francis and Uncle Sven. Vivian sat to Uncle Sven's right.

"Your voice has improved, brother," Evelyn said, trying to lighten the moment.

"What a dreadful thing to say," Sven said. "You know very well my recording was nonpareil."

"You mean non-listenable?" his sister said.

"*Not at all*," Sven feigned offense. "I got a letter from Caruso."

"Begging you never to sing again," Evelyn said.

Sven forced an insulted expression. "How cruel," he said. "How uninformed."

"Recording, Uncle?" Mary asked.

"*You didn't know?*" Sven looked aghast. "I would have thought they'd play the record for you night and day. How remiss of them."

"When did you record it?" Mary asked.

"In my callow youth," Sven said.

"In the United States?"

"No, no," Sven told her. "Norway. The recording capital of the world."

"Oslo?" she asked.

"It was called Christiana in those days," Sven told her.

"How did it go, Uncle?"

"*Sensationally.*" Sven said. "Number One on the Norsky Hit Parade."

"How did it *go,*" Mary repeated.

"You shouldn't have asked him that," Evelyn said.

"Well, let's see," Sven said, ignoring her. He cleared his throat, loudly. "Me-me-me-me-me! That should do it."

He began to sing the Norwegian Song. It was a bouncy, hyperactive melody. Evelyn made a face and covered her ears. Francis stifled a laugh. Vivian did the same, holding onto her nose. Bob and Mary snickered uncontrollably. Fanny and Gladys reacted with smiles, Gladys shaking her head.

Sven finished the song and looked around the table. "No applause?" he said. "No cheers?"

Bob clapped his hands. "Bravo, Uncle!" he said.

"Encore?" Sven asked.

"No!" Vivian cried. Everyone laughed. "I mean, no thank you." Vivian added.

Sven chuckled and shook his head. "From the very lips of my niece," he said with false gloom. "Oh, well, she's young. She hasn't acquired artistic appreciation yet." He directed a somber look at Vivian. "When I performed my song at the Christiana Opera House—"

"The *Opera House?*" Evelyn cut him off.

"Well, I was *supposed* to perform it there," Sven went on. "With my dance, of course."

"Your *dance?*" Evelyn had difficulty keeping a straight face. Her mouth fell open as her brother stood up. "Oh, *no,*" she said.

"There'll be only cheers when you see it," Sven said.

"Or vomiting," Vivian said.

"*Sister,*" said her mother. Everyone was abruptly quiet. "Apologize to Uncle Sven," Evelyn said.

Vivian's lips tightened.

"*Sister,*" her mother warned.

"She was only joking," Fanny said, anxious to make peace.

"*Hush,* girls," Sven said. "You're about to see Nijinsky dance!"

Singing the song again, he commenced a shuffling, twisting dance, frowning as everyone exploded with laughter. "You're failing to grasp the quality of this," he said.

He continued singing and dancing, his slow movements becoming more exaggerated by the moment. Bob, then Francis, began to applaud in rhythm.

"*Now you're getting it*," Sven said. He was getting breathless.

"That's enough, Sven," Evelyn sounded concerned.

Sven finished the song and dance and sat back down, breathing heavily. "Bravo, Uncle Sven!" Bob told him. "Bravo," Francis said. "Very good," Vivian told him. Evelyn gave her an approving look.

"I'm not the man I was," Sven observed, taking in a deep breath.

"Sure you are," Bob told him. "Nijinsky would be green with envy. Bravo, again." Everyone added their own manner of praise, most of it tongue-in-cheek.

"That was…*breathtaking*, brother," Evelyn said.

"I knew you'd come around," Sven said. He drew in a long gasp of air. "Breathtaking is the word." An amused sound ran around the table.

"All right. Now that *that's* out of the way," Evelyn said.

"*Out of the way?*" Sven was still stabilizing his breathing. "Shame, shame, Evelina."

She smiled at her brother, lovingly; then looked at Bob. "Have some cake, Robert," she said. "A sandwich. Some coffee?" She glanced at Sven. "Less singing?" she said.

"*Uh*," Sven reacted. Bob grinned. "Do you have some soda in the house?" he asked. "Coke? Pepsi?"

Evelyn turned to her son. "Franny, get Uncle Bob a Pepsi Cola. You want ice, Bob?"

"Not if it's cold," Bob said.

"I think we have some in the ice box," Evelyn grimaced. "*Refrigerator*," she corrected herself. "Franny?"

"Okay," Francis stood and moved toward the kitchen.

"Fanny," Sven said.

"Frances," she replied.

"What?" Sven asked.

Francis turned back and said, "What?" at the same time.

"I changed my name," Fanny explained.

"*Why*?" Sven asked.

"Confusing," Francis said, moving into the kitchen.

"You changed your name to that of your nephew?" Sven asked.

"No, no," fanny told him. "E-s, not *I*-s."

"*Why*?" Sven asked again. "What's wrong with Fanny?"

"Well…" his sister seemed to feel a little flustered. "It's not a nice word anymore."

"You're right," Sven said. "*Terrible* word. I don't like my name either. From now on, I'm Ethelbert."

"You're silly," Fanny told him.

"No, no. Ethelbert. Norway's paramount recording star."

"You should write a book about yourself, Uncle," Bob said.

"Tried that," Sven replied. He inclined his head toward Richard. "Your Big Shot Hollywood writer there told me I didn't know what I was doing."

"Oh, my God, *two* of you now?" Richard said, half seriously. Mary looked displeased. "What I did," he explained to his brother, "was edit a few lines and tell Uncle that he should include the toast story."

"That's not all he did," Sven said. There was no humor in his voice.

"I thought it was, Uncle Sven," Richard said defensively.

"The toast story?" Mary asked.

"It should be in there," Fanny said.

"It never will be," Sven said. Now he sounded aggravated. "Since the book will never be published."

"Oh, come on, Uncle," Richard said. "Don't say that. I didn't say anything bad about your story."

"Story?" said Sven. "I thought it was real."

"The *toast* story?" Vivian snapped.

"Oh…okay," Richard conceded. "When I was a kid—three or four, I guess—I had to spend the night at Uncle's house."

"I needed to go to Alicia's house," Fanny broke in, explaining. "She wasn't feeling well."

"She was busy gaining weight," Sven said.

"Now stop that," Evelyn told him. Sven didn't reply.

"*Anyway*," Richard said.

"Yes, *anyway*," Bob said. "Time for the world-famous toast story."

"Uncle made me breakfast the next morning," Richard went on, smiling. "I guess Aunt Ella wasn't there.

"She *wasn't*," Sven said. His tone was grim.

"*Anyway*," Richard continued. "I told Uncle he was making the breakfast wrong, he wasn't scraping the toast. Mom always—"

"Not *always*!" Fanny protested, laughing.

"*Usually*," Richard said. "Mom *usually* burned the toast."

"Well, the toaster didn't work very well," Fanny said. "One of those stove top ones."

"*Anyway*," Richard tried again. "When Mom burned the toast she always scraped off the burned part. So I assumed it was the way toast was made. And I told Uncle—"

He broke off. Everyone stared at him.

"Well, it was funny at the time," he said. "I was only three."

"Four," said his mother. "I wouldn't have taken you to your Uncle's house if you were only three."

Silence at the table.

"Now you know why I didn't put the toast story in my book," Sven said. It wasn't a joke, but everyone laughed.

Francis returned from the kitchen with a bottle of Pepsi Cola. He handed it to Bob who thanked him and shook off Evelyn's offer of a glass. "I'll just use the bottle," he said.

He took a sip, then, as the silence lasted, said to Sven, "Uncle, I don't think Richard was necessarily correcting you."

"I need *correcting*?" Sven challenged.

"Of course not," Richard said. "You know what I mean."

"Not exactly," Sven said.

Silence again. Evelyn started to speak, then broke off as Sven spoke first. Aware of the tension he'd created, his tone was light again.

"Anyway, Fanny—I refuse to call you Frances lest it confuse your nephew—Why bother changing your name at all? Doesn't Evelina call you Fasa?"

Fanny's smile was thin. "It's only a nickname," she said.

"—which means?" Bob asked.

"*Fusspot,*" Vivian told him.

"*Sister,*" her mother said.

"I'm not your sister," Vivian lashed out.

Francis looked at her in surprise. Evelyn looked startled at the vehemence in her daughter's voice. She strained for control. "I know that," she said. "My sister is Fasa," she added, trying in vain for humor. Seeing that no one was smiling, she said to Vivian, "And what you said Fasa means... I don't know what it means exactly. What I told you was just a guess. *And a joke,*" she added quickly to her sister.

"Some joke," Fanny said, trying to sound amused.

"It *was* a joke, Fasa—Fanny—Frances," Evelyn said. "Okay?"

"*Thank* you," Fanny said.

Evelyn clearly thought that her sister's thank you was genuine and managed a smile. "You're *welcome,*" she said. "*Now*...let's talk about something else."

"How about the *funeral*?" Vivian said.

"Well...*yes,*" Evelyn said, not certain why her daughter suggested it. "The funeral then. Let's discuss the funeral."

"Sounds like fun," Sven said.

Evelyn's lips tightened. "Well, that's why we're here, isn't it, brother?" The hostess warmth had vanished from her voice. She willed it back. "Fanny—Frances—*both* of us thought the service was beautiful. Especially Mister Armbruster's' speech."

"Was he that skinny little shrimp with orange hair?" Sven asked. Everyone but Fanny and Evelyn laughed.

"He isn't *skinny,*" Evelyn said, looking at her son and daughter in disapproval.

"And his hair is not orange," Fanny said.

"Well, it looked orange to me," Sven told his sister. "It was badly dyed, anyway."

"It was a lovely speech," Evelyn insisted.

Sven's voice grew high-pitched and nasal as he ranted, "The comforting warmth of divine spirit has now embraced Bertolf in its arms of blah-blah-blah."

Francis and Vivian cracked up, Evelyn scowling at them. Fanny, despite amusement, gave them an admonishing look. Bob and Mary had difficulty restraining their amusement. Sven looked innocent.

"Very funny," Evelyn said.

"He failed to comfort me," Sven told her.

"It was a good speech," Evelyn said.

"*Lovely*," Vivian said in a flat voice. Her mother gave her a look. Francis started to grin, then repressed it.

"By the way," Bob said. "Who suggested the open casket?"

"*We* did," Evelyn said firmly. "We thought it was a good way for everyone to say good-bye to Bert."

"*You*, thought," Vivian said. "Franny and I had nothing to do with it."

Evelyn's expression hardened as she looked at her daughter.

"It *was* a little ghoulish, Tante," Bob told her.

"*Ghoulish*? Goodness gracious, Robert," she made a clucking noise. "Your sister thought it was grotesque. We had—" she glanced at Vivian, "*Tollef and I* had no idea it would be so disturbing."

"*You* had no idea," Vivian said. "Pop had nothing to do with it." Evelyn sighed heavily. "*All right*, sister." Hurriedly she added, "*I* know. You're not my sister. It's just a nickname."

"*I don't like it*," Vivian said. Evelyn sighed again.

"When I made arrangements for the service," Bob said, "nothing was said about the casket. So I assumed—"

"I'm *sorry*," Evelyn broke in. "I didn't mean to go over your head."

"You *didn't*, Tante," Bob assured her. "You were just doing what you thought was right."

"I *was*," Evelyn said, dabbing at her eyes.

"Now there's nothing to cry about," Bob said, his smile was gentle.

"*I'm not crying*," she muttered.

"She's always crying," Vivian said.

Evelyn drew in a sniffling breath. "*Oh*," she said. "Just...stop."

"Give your mother a break, Viv," Bob said. Vivian exhaled loudly. "She doesn't mean it, Mom," Francis said. "I know," his mother responded. Vivian cast her eyes to heaven.

"Why don't we talk about Pop?" Bob suggested. "That *is* why we're here."

"Why not indeed?" Sven nodded.

"He was a true gentleman," Bob said.

"Yes, he was," Evelyn said. She looked at her sister. Fanny said nothing.

"And *generous*," Bob said. He looked across the table at his aunt. "Didn't he keep your family going during the Depression?" he asked.

"Well...he helped," Evelyn sounded reluctant. "But all of us worked as well. Tollef cleaned offices. I cleaned houses. Vivian worked in the Five and Ten. Francis delivered newspapers."

"But Pop helped keep you financially afloat." Bob said. It was not a question.

"He *helped*." Evelyn seemed unwilling to admit any more.

"Bert *was* a generous man," Sven said. "If I needed to borrow money, I got it. He was definitely a generous man."

"And a *drinking* man," Fanny was unable to keep it in.

Bob's voice tightened as he said, "Mom, he had to entertain the captain's of ships he bought supplies from."

"*Supplies*," she said. "You mean *liquor*."

"*It was Prohibition, Mom*," Bob said. "There were only so many ways to earn money."

"Hold on, you're losing me," Sven said.

"Mom never told you?" Bob asked.

"I most certainly did not," Fanny said.

"*Why?*" Bob asked.

"Because I was *ashamed*," his mother said.

"Well, *I was proud*," Bob said, his face beginning redden a bit.

"Daddy," Mary warned him

"Well, I *was* proud," Bob declared. "I *am* proud. The money Pop made supplying five speakeasy's in the Wall Street area, kept us all going."

"I didn't know that," Francis said, impressed.

"*Five speakeasy's*," Vivian said. It was impossible to tell if she was critical or impressed.

"Intriguing," Sven said. "*Five* of them."

"*Shameful*," Fanny said.

"*No it wasn't*, Mom!" Bob stormed.

"We didn't know about it," Evelyn said. "If we had, we wouldn't have accepted any money."

"You *did* know," Vivian said. "I heard you and Pop talking about it."

"*Sister*," her mother interrupted. She grimaced, gritting her teeth. "*Vivian, please*."

"Well...*nuts*," Vivian said. "The truth is the truth."

"It's too bad it all came up," Fanny said.

"Well, you *brought* it up, Mom," Bob told her.

"*I did not*," his mother flared.

"Mom, was it such a crime what Pop did?" Bob demanded.

"It *was* a crime, Bob," Gladys said.

"*No*," Sven said, almost pleadingly. This joke fell flat.

"*Yes*, Uncle," Gladys insisted. "He could have gone to prison. We could have *all* gone to prison!"

"Oh, I doubt that," Bob said.

"Well, *don't* doubt it, damn it!" Gladys suddenly erupted.

"*Gladys*," her mother said, her voice pained. It wasn't clear whether she was complaining about the language or not.

"*Well...Mom*," Gladys protested. "You know Bob always acts as though he knows everything! Well, he *doesn't*!"

"Sorry, sis," Bob said.

"Oh...*poo*," Gladys replied. Grudgingly.

"That puts me in my place," Bob said.

"Poos you in your place," Sven corrected. Francis chuckled and Vivian smiled. No one else seemed amused.

A polite silence was ended when Fanny said, "It's how your father learned to drink."

"*Mom*," Bob pleaded.

"Well, it *was*," his mother refused to back down.

"Fanny—Frances—Fasa—Fusspot," Sven said. "You know us Vikings don't have to learn to drink. It's in our blood."

"How well I remember," Fanny said.

"*Ooh.* Touché, good sister," Sven said. "If you're referring to me, that is."

"If the bottle fits," Fanny told him. Sven laughed. "Touché, again," he said.

"Anyway, what you say isn't true," Fanny told him. "Bert didn't drink when we met."

Sven responded in Norwegian. "You are a truly naïve child," he said. Fanny stiffened. "When he was working under me at the shipyard," Sven continued in English, "Did he often come home late at night and tell you we were *working* late?"

Fanny remained silent.

"We were at *Ole's Bar & Grill* downing a few snorts while we were chatting," Sven said, adding, "A *few*, mind you."

"So he learned from you, as well," Fanny said bitterly.

"*Fanny*," Sven said. "For God's sake." he added in Norwegian.

"For God's sake, Sven?" Fanny sounded pained and angry at once. "That you and the captain's introduced Bert to the Devil's Brew?"

"*Fanny*," Sven sounded incredulous.

"*Are you serious*?" Bob said. "*The Devil's Brew*?"

"*I am serious*," his mother told him.

"Mom, that's *ridiculous*," Bob said.

"*Not quite*," Gladys objected.

"Oh, Mom is serious all right," Richard told his brother. "She saw a bottle of vodka in our kitchen cupboard once and said the same thing."

"Good lord," Bob muttered.

Fanny lost control. "It *is* The Devil's Brew!" she cried. "It destroys lives! It destroyed mine! All I wanted was to go back to school and finish my education! He said absolutely not!"

Bob looked confused. "Mom, what does that have to do with him drinking?"

"He didn't *think* right when he was drinking!" she said loudly. "It made him stubborn! *Selfish*!"

Abruptly, she was crying.

"Oh, *Fanny. Frances*," Evelyn said.

"You don't have to call me that," Fanny told her in a sobbing voice. "It's too hard to remember."

Bob got up and moved around to his mother. He put an arm around her shoulders. "It's all right, Mom," he said. "Don't cry. We're sorry."

"I'm not," Sven said. A soft, wheezy laughter circled the table.

"What made you marry Pop in the first place?" Bob asked.

Fanny's continued crying became half laughter. "Because he was so *handsome*! I fell head over heels."

She corrected herself immediately. "I was *young*," she said. "I had no sense."

"Well, he *was* handsome," Evelyn said.

"How old *were* you, Mom?" Mary asked.

"Not old enough," Fanny told her daughter-in-law. "Barely sixteen."

"My lord," Mary said.

"He was twenty-eight," Fanny went on. "A man of the world."

"Well, hardly that," Sven said resisting a smile.

"I'm sorry I upset you, Mom," Bob told her. "I didn't mean to."

Fanny reached up and patted his cheek.

"That's all right," she said. Bob leaned over and kissed her on the cheek, then sat down again. Evelyn had been standing since her sister began to cry. Now she sat down as well.

"I know something you don't know about your father," Sven said to Bob.

"Oh?" Bob's smile was curious.

"We know he was in the Norwegian Merchant Marines," Sven said.

"Yes, I *did* know," Bob replied.

"Did you know he was a skiing champion in Norway?"

"*No*," Bob grinned. "That I didn't know. I wonder why he never told us."

"He told *me*," Gladys broke in.

"He *did*?" Bob reacted in surprise. "When?"

"When I was in a bar with him," Gladys answered.

"*Gladys*," Fanny sounded shocked.

"Mom, *I was a little girl*," Gladys told her tensely.

"And drinking already," Sven said. He chuckled somberly.

Gladys response was only half serious. "I had a lemonade, Uncle."

"One of the most *pernicious* drinks in the universe," Sven said gravely.

"Oh, stop it, Sven," Evelyn told him.

"As you say, Evelina," Sven agreed.

Gladys wasn't finished. "I know something else about Pop that nobody else knows," she said. "Not even Mom."

"He was a German spy in World War Two," Sven supplied.

"*Sven*," Evelyn cautioned him. He raised his arms in surrender. "*Kamerad*," he said.

Gladys ignored him. "*He was a ladies man*," she said.

Dead silence in the room. Evelyn broke it first. "*No*," she said. It wasn't clear whether she was sincere or not.

"What makes you say that?" Bob asked his sister.

"Yes, what?" Fanny said in a thin voice.

"When I was in the bar with him, he flirted with two different women," Gladys said.

"That was it?" Bob said. "*Flirted* with two women?"

"*Outrageous*," Sven said. It was a poorly rendered joke.

"*I was there*," Gladys eyed her brother angrily.

"And if I had been there, I might have flirted with them too!" Bob said. "It's a male tradition, Gladys, flirting in bar rooms."

"*It was more than flirting*," Gladys said tightly.

"You said *flirting*," Bob challenged.

Again, she erupted in anger. "What was I supposed to say? That he *came on* to them? He *did*!"

"With his little girl next to him?" Bob demanded.

"*Yes*!" she raged. "*Exactly*!"

"I doubt it," Bob said.

"*You weren't there*!" Gladys shouted.

"Children!" Fanny begged. No one heard her.

"I *lived* with him, Gladys!" Bob tried to control his temper but succeeded only partially. "For *two years*! And I never saw him being a ladies man! Not *once*!"

"He wouldn't have been in front of you," Gladys said.

"Oh, but he did in front of you!" Bob said. "His *little* girl!"

"*Daddy!*" Mary cautioned again.

"*All right*," Bob said, glancing at her for a second.

"Oh, well," Gladys gave up. "The hell with it."

"*Please*, Gladys," Fanny said. It *was* the language after all.

"What I *did* see," Bob said. "Was that his heart was broken because Mom put him out of the house."

"Oh, that's not fair, Robert," his mother said.

"Isn't it?" he countered.

"*No.*" Now she was angry. "We *separated*. I didn't *put* him out of the house."

"He didn't see it that way, Mom," Bob told her. "You put him out of the house. He said it a hundred times."

"I had two children, Robert! I couldn't raise them married to a man who drank!" She sounded close to tears again. It made her voice tremble.

Bob refused to give up. Even when Mary tapped him on the shoulder; he gave her a hard look when she did. "He drank when we lived together because he was unhappy," he said to his mother. "You took his life away when you told him to leave."

"I *never*—" Fanny began.

Bob wouldn't let her finish. "He loved living in Allendale with you, Gladys and me," he looked at Richard. "He would have loved living with you as well if he hadn't been put out of the house before you were born."

"Oh, *Robert*," his mother said unhappily.

"He led a Boy Scout Troop I was in," Bob told his brother. "He took us all skiing in the winter—he never mentioned that he was a champion in Norway. He went swimming with us in the summer. He took us out to dinner."

Fanny's voice was bitter. "Apparently, I put a saint out of the house," she said.

"No, not a saint, but a kind, generous man," Bob told her. "A man who'd lost everything. When I was living with him he was pleasant and good-natured. Even *funny*, do you remember how funny Pop could be?"

his voice shook a little as he finished. "He didn't feel too funny when I was with him. His heart was broken."

He slumped back in his chair, forcing a smile as Mary patted his hand. Francis and Vivian looked at him with new interest. They'd never heard him talk like that before.

"Was he *so* bad, Fanny?" Sven asked. There was no humor in his voice anymore.

"He *drank*, Sven," his sister answered. "A *good deal*."

"*So did I*," Sven admitted. "But I stopped."

"*He didn't*," she said.

"Well, isn't this interesting?" Evelyn said. She sounded dubious.

"Yes," Francis said. He meant it.

"Could be," Vivian said. Her mother looked at her questioningly.

"I didn't know you had a drinking problem, Uncle," Bob said.

"Oh, it wasn't a problem, I enjoyed it," Sven told him. Francis was unable to stifle an explosive laugh. Sven sighed. "Runs in the family, seems like," he said.

"Well, not entirely," Bob denied.

"You don't think you have a problem, do you?" his uncle said.

Bob tensed a little, forced a smile. "Nothing I can't control," he said.

"That's what I said, too," Sven told him.

"Well, you *did* stop," Bob reminded him.

"*I did*," Sven said, indicating that the subject was concluded.

Bob held on to it, asking his mother. "Don't you think Pop would have stopped if you'd asked him?"

"You think I *didn't* ask him?" she said.

"And he never tried?" Bob asked.

"No, Robert, no."

"He told me he would have," Bob said.

"He wasn't telling you the truth," she claimed.

"*Mom, he told me that you never asked him to stop drinking!*"

"I *did*," she cried. "A *hundred times*!" Her cheeks were reddening.

"Okay, okay," Bob tried to end the conflict. "Let's just say you couldn't get through to each other."

"That's for sure," Fanny said grimly.

"All right," Bob responded. "I accept that."

"You *accept* that?" Vivian snapped. "What are you? The judge and jury?"

Bob looked at her in surprise. They'd never had an exchange before. "No, Vivian," he said patiently. "Just trying to get at the truth."

"Vivian returned his friendly smile. "I'm all for that," she said.

"Good," Bob said. "*Good.*"

"Let's talk about something else," Evelyn suggested uncomfortably.

"*Good*," Sven said. "Who shall we eviscerate now?"

"*Sven*," Fanny appealed to him.

"I wasn't attacking anyone, Uncle," Bob explained. "I was just defending my father. He can't defend *himself* now. And he was a *good man*." His voice cracked a little. "He loved his family. He took good care of them." His voice cracked all the way. "He was my scout leader for chrissake!"

"It's all right, Bob," Fanny reassured him.

Sven looked at Bob, his tongue firmly back in cheek again. "I accept that," he said. Glanced at Vivian, "No comment?" he asked. Her lips only tightened. "So who do we attack now?" Sven asked. "Evelina was right. This *is* interesting. Though I doubt if she really meant it."

"Now you stop it," Evelyn said.

"How about *you*, Uncle?" Vivian's smile was not a pleasant one.

"Well...*why not?*" Sven agreed. "I submit myself to the mercy of the tribunal. Attack away."

"Your singing is awful," Evelyn said.

"That's an old attack, Evelina," Sven told her. "And undoubtedly true. Come up with something new."

"Give me time," Evelyn told him.

"Granted," Sven said. "Anyone else?"

"*How about Mary*," Richard broke in.

"*Whoa*," Mary said. "Where did that come from?"

"I'm tired of this Hollywood Big Shot routine," Richard said.

"Oh...well," Mary mumbled.

"I thought about it while I was flying here," Richard said.

"First class, of course," Mary said.

"No, *in my private jet*," Richard slammed back.

"I believe it," Mary said.

Bob's voice was gentle. "Come on, Mar," he said.

"I was flying coach, Mary," Richard told her. "The way I *always* fly. I can't afford First Class."

"*Sure*," she said.

"You want to look at my ticket?" he demanded.

"I'll look at it," she said.

"Mar, *come on*," Bob told her.

"If I fly First Class," Richard spoke irritably, "*which is almost never*; it's because the Studio I'm working for pays for it."

"Can we go home?" Mary asked her husband.

"*Why?*" he wanted to know.

"What's the matter, Mary?" Richard asked. "*The truth stick in your throat?*"

Mary stood up. "I'm going!" she said.

"*Why?*" Bob asked again. "Has he said anything so awful?"

"*Like the truth sticking in my throat?*" she answered angrily.

"Your wife doesn't like me, Bob," his brother said. "She never has. I don't know why."

"I'm not sure that's true, Dick," Bob said. He looked at Mary. "Sid-down, Mar," he added.

"I'm *going home*," she said.

"Oh, for chrissake, *sit down!*" Bob ordered. Mary sat.

"Let's talk about something else," Evelyn said, too softly to be heard.

"Let's not and say we did," Vivian said. She'd taken note of her mother's plaintive request.

Mary spoke then. "You say I've always disliked you," she said to Richard. "Not true. You were a darling little boy."

"*Yes, he was*," Fanny said.

"Oh, hush up, Fasa," Evelyn told her.

"For a *while*," Mary amended. "Then you became a royal pain in the ass."

Fanny winced. "I prefer darling little boy," Evelyn said. "*Amen*," Fanny seconded.

"Oh, hush up, Fasa," Vivian said. "You too, Evelina." They looked at her with startled disapproval.

Richard was grinning. "A royal pain in the ass?"

"*Richard*," Fanny muttered.

"Yes," Mary said, unable to completely suppress an amused smile. "You remember your sixth birthday party? Your mother made you a banana shortcake, which you loved. You have an enormous slice of it and, when it fell over, you started to cry like a baby."

"So?" Richard looked and sounded confused now.

"Your mother told all of us—" Mary started.

"*Suggested*," Fanny broke in, knowing what Mary was about to say.

"No, *told* all of us to knock over *our* slices to make little Dicky feel better."

Vivian snickered. "You mean Dicky Bird," she said.

"So we did," Mary continued. "And you started laughing."

"*What-a-pain-in-the-ass*," Richard said. "I should have been shot."

"You should have been," Mary agreed.

"That was it?" Bob queried his wife. "I remember that too. It hardly qualified Dick to be a royal pain in the—" he glanced at his mother. "Poopy-doop," he finished. She managed a smile.

"*Poopy-doop?*" Mary asked.

"Mom's medical term for the rear-end," Bob told her.

Mary smiled, then looked back at Richard accusingly. "There was more, though. Lot's more. You always had to have your own way. *Always*. If you didn't get it, you either screamed like a banshee—"

"He never screamed," Fanny said, determinedly.

"*Or*," Mary went on, "pouted for the rest of the day."

"*No*," Fanny said.

"Yes, I think so," Sven broke in.

"Mom, you know it's true," Mary said. "You never told him to stop."

"That's true," Francis agreed.

"Whoa!" Richard said. "You're all ganging up on me now. I must *really* have been a pain in the—poopy-doop."

"The *ass*," Vivian said.

"*Sister*," Evelyn cut in.

"I'm not your sister," Vivian told her. "I have never been your sister. I will never *be* your sister. *Got* it?"

Evelyn sighed deeply. "I give up," she said.

"You never have before," Vivian told her.

Silence. Followed by Fanny's predictable defense. "Anyway Mary, Richard was such a sweet boy most of the time."

"You never told him to stop," Mary reminded her.

"*I tried*," Gladys said.

"Now you're *all* against me," Richard said. His smile was strained.

"There *is* some truth to what's being said," Bob told her.

"Now it's *everybody*," Richard said, protesting lightly. "Call the F.B.I. Toss me in the clink."

"The what?" Francis asked.

"The prison, jail," Richard told his cousin.

"Oh," Francis said. "How about the electric chair?"

"*Oh!*" Richard feigned repulsion. "Some pal you are." Francis laughed.

Richard looked across the table. "Why didn't you ever say anything?" he asked Mary.

"In front of your mother?" Mary said. "Come on."

"Mary, I was just a kid," Richard was defensive now. "A spoiled kid; granted. My mother should have whacked me over the bean with a frying pan."

"I couldn't do that," Fanny said, seriously.

"I could have," Vivian said.

"Another pal," Richard said to her.

"I told you about it," Gladys told her mother. "You paid no attention to me."

"Or me," Bob said. "I mentioned it, too."

"Most of the time he was so *sweet*." Fanny protested.

"Did that excuse his tantrums?" Mary asked.

"*They weren't tantrums*," Fanny claimed.

"*Yes, they were*, Mom," Mary argued. "Very ugly tantrums."

"Dear God," Richard said. "I must have been a rotten little bastard."

"Now you've got it," Sven told him with his usual make-believe seriousness. At the same time Fanny said, "*Dick*," commenting on his language.

"Sorry, Mom," he said. "It just slipped out."

"Then there were the lousy little drawings," Mary went on. Richard's groan melodramatic. "Your crumby little poems. Your idiotic stories about—hell, I don't know, good-hearted squirrels or something."

Richard and Bob started laughing together. So did Francis and Vivian and Uncle Sven. Evelyn wasn't sure how to react, Fanny was. "They were cute," she said.

"Yes, they were," Evelyn supported.

"No, they weren't, Mom," Mary said. "And we had to look at every lousy drawing and read or listen to every lousy poem and story. And tell little Dicky Boy how wonderful they were, how talented he was."

"He *was* talented," Fanny persisted. "He *is* talented. Look how he makes his living."

"As a Hollywood Big Shot?" Mary said.

"Oh, for chrissake, shut up!" Richard said, still laughing.

Mary started laughing, too. "Well, isn't it true?" she demanded.

"*No!*" Richard cried. "I get fifteen-hundred dollars for a half-hour script! I get twenty-five hundred if I adapt one of my own published stories. None of which goes very far to support a wife and two kids. I can hardly be called a Hollywood Big Shot."

Mary looked chastened. "I didn't know," she murmured. "I thought you made a lot more."

"*I told you*," Bob reminded her. She nodded curtly.

"Never-the-less, I apologize for all the aggravation I put you through when I was a rotten little kid," Richard said to Mary.

"It was entertaining," she replied, attempting to make peace.

"No, it wasn't," Bob said, holding a droll smile. "You were a pain in the ass." Fanny tightened at the word.

"I'm sure I was," Richard agreed. He stood up; he circled the table and extended his hands toward Mary. Surprised but pleased, Mary made no move.

"*Mar*," Bob urged. She hesitated, then put out her hands and let Richard pull her to her feet. He gave her a hug. "I'm sorry," he said. "I didn't know. I was just a dumb kid."

Mary hugged him back. "You're forgiven," she said.

"Bless you," Richard told her, smilingly.

Sven spoke with the intonation of a radio announcer. "And so another family rift is healed before our very eyes, our very ears. Tune in tomorrow for another episode of—" he finished in Norwegian: "*Norsky Crap*."

"You're terrible," Fanny said, trying not to smile.

"Don't forget you haven't had your turn yet," Vivian said.

"Trapped again," Sven said.

"You're really on a tear," Bob said to Vivian, amused.

"A what?" she asked.

"You're out for blood," he said.

Her smile was difficult to assess. "Maybe," she said. Evelyn looked at her uneasily.

"I just thought of something else about Pop," Gladys said. "Something nobody's mentioned."

"Oh, dear," Fanny said.

"No, no, it's not something bad, Mom," Gladys said. "It's probably funny."

"We could use funny," Sven said.

"Just hang on," Evelyn told him. "We'll get to you, yet."

"*Yes, we will*," Vivian pronounced.

"Oy," Sven said. He looked at Gladys. "So tell us, niece. We'll decide if it's bad or not."

"Pop used to fry bacon," Gladys began.

"Doesn't sound bad so far," Sven said.

Gladys ignored him. "He didn't like sliced bacon," she said. "He preferred to fry it in chunks."

"Now *that's* bad," Sven said.

"Hush," Evelyn told him.

"Yes, sis," he said.

"After the bacon chunks were fried," Gladys went on. "Pop would pour the left-over fat into a small bowl."

"Now we're getting somewhere," Sven said.

"*Brother!*" Evelyn warned.

"*Yes*, sis?" Sven asked.

"Fermay La Bush," she said.

"La Bush is fermayed," Sven assured her.

"Proceed, Gladys," Evelyn said. "We'll keep your uncle under wraps."

"Thank you," Gladys said. "*Anyway—*"

"*Anyway,*" Sven said

"*Svennington!*" Evelyn growled. Sven pointed at his mouth. "Fermayed, fermayed," he said. He mimicked zipping shut his lips.

"Continuing," Gladys said. "I hope."

She looked questioningly at her uncle who pretended to zip shut his lips repeatedly. She snickered, shaking her head, then proceeded with her story.

"Pop liked to eat week-old pumpernickel. He'd cut off an end slice…the *scalken* I think it was called."

Fanny smiled. "That's right," she said.

"Then he'd spread—*thickly*—on the *scalken*—the hardened bacon fat."

"You're kidding," Sven said.

"*No*," Bob told him grinning. I saw him do it."

"Then sprinkle it—*heavily*—with *pepper!*—for *breakfast!*" Gladys said.

"*No*," Francis said.

"*Yes!*" Bob said, laughing.

"*Peppered, hard bacon grease on stale pumpernickel,*" Gladys said, laughing. "It had to look *revolting*. It must have *tasted* revolting."

"It *did*," Fanny said laughing uncontrollably.

"*Yuck,*" Vivian said.

"It *was* revolting!" Bob said, still laughing. "I tried it once. *Revolting*." He shook his head, amused by his mother's laughter. "But Pop *loved* it."

"Yes, he did," Gladys said. "He'd wash it down with black coffee so thick a half dollar could have floated on it."

"Cowboy coffee," Richard said. No one paid attention.

"It's all true," Fanny said, her laughter now reduced to a chuckle.

"No further comment, Brother?" Evelyn asked.

"So completes the intimate portrait of Bertolf Mathiesen, Norwegian Bacon Consumer," Sven remarked. Everyone laughed.

"Well, now that that's all done, why doesn't everyone have something to eat?" Evelyn invited.

"No more attacks?" Vivian said.

"No, dear. No more attacks," her mother said.

"For *now*," Sven said. "I'm still on the rack."

"I'll wait," Vivian said.

"*Intermission*," Evelyn announced over her.

intermission

If this were a stage play—which I hope it will be someday—there would be a break in the story but not a standard theatre intermission. There would be no closing of a curtain, no dimming of lights. Instead, the play would continue. The nine performers would have a snack, rising, one by one to pick up plates and silverware, make themselves sandwiches, spoon on cole slaw and/or potato salad, pour themselves coffee or enter the kitchen for milk or soda, opening and shutting the off-stage refrigerator. They would remain in character, continuing the play but on a less informative level, perhaps providing, in some ways, subtle insights into their personalities.

The nine would remain on stage, sitting around the huge round table. They would continue conversing, but reveal nothing of import, chatting idly about the food being eaten, the juice, soda, Postum or coffee being drunk.

The audience, if they chose, could leave the theatre, purchase a drink, have a smoke or go to the bathroom. They would miss nothing vital to the story because nothing vital is being spoken on the stage. So it is in this never-occurring event. Digestion—and irrelevant comments regarding the world dominate the stage. This novel, as well, if one chooses to call it that.

Presently, a bell would ring, a gong would chime, a buzzer sound announces the main body of the story about to proceed. So too, my mythical account.

act two

"Why don't we talk about something pleasant now?" Evelyn suggested.

"*No*," Francis and Vivian said at the same moment.

Evelyn looked at them in surprise. "*Both* of you?" she said.

"Me anyway," Francis said.

"*And me*," Vivian added.

"Wait a minute!" Sven broke in with feigned bristling. "One at a time here! Sven Svennington is entitled to his evisceration first."

"Well said, Uncle," Bob told him.

"Thank you, nephew," Sven responded.

"Well, I give up," Evelyn said. "Line up folks. Uncle Sven first. Then…who?"

"*Me*," Vivian said.

"Or me," Francis added.

"*Fine*," Evelyn said; her cheeks were flushed. "Then Bob, then Mary, then Fasa, then me. Let's make a night of it."

"Evelina," Fanny chided her.

"No, no, let's keep this going," Evelyn said. "You first, brother. What's your problem?"

"I have a sister who refuses to remain quiet," Sven answered.

Evelyn imitated her lip zipping pretense.

"That's good," Sven told her. "Where did you get that interesting little movement?"

"From a brother who has even more trouble remaining quiet," Evelyn said.

"Touché, dear sister," Sven said in Norwegian. He looked around the table. "All right, fire away!" he invited.

"What about your wife?" Vivian asked.

Sven got up. "Time to go," he said.

"No, you don't," Vivian dared him. "Tante Fanny didn't back off."

"Tante Fanny is a blabbermouth," Sven said.

They all made a negative sound. Sven clucked. "Tante Fanny is *not* a blabbermouth then," he said. "She is a non-revealing mute."

He sat down.

"Talking about non-revealing, Uncle," Richard said, "I asked you why Lily wasn't here and you said she wasn't sick. Why *isn't* she here?"

"You sure you want to know?" Sven asked. There was no humor in his voice.

To his surprise, Bob, Mary, Francis and Vivian all shouted, *"Yes!"*

Sven winced. "Swamped by the majority," he said.

"So?" Richard said.

To everyone's surprise, Sven's expression grew sour "We're not on speaking terms," he told them.

"How come, Uncle?" Bob asked.

"Because I criticized her," Sven explained.

"What about?" Bob probed.

"Are you *sure* you want to know?" Sven asked. He was completely serious now.

"Yes, Uncle. *Yes,"* Bob told him.

"You may be sorry you asked," Sven said.

"Try us, Uncle," Mary said. Francis and Vivian remained still as though worried that they'd brought up a subject they shouldn't have. Fanny and Evelyn looked uneasy.

"Very well," Sven said. He conveyed a different Uncle image now; grimly conscious of something he wished had remained secret.

"What did you criticize Lily about?" Bob persisted.

There was a long pause in Sven's answer. When he finally did speak, it was with great reluctance. "Her husband's suicide," he murmured.

"My God," Mary said. "We never heard about that."

"Neither did we," Gladys told her uncle.

"*Sven*," Fanny said. "We didn't know."

"Then I'm sorry I brought it up," Sven said.

"We didn't know because no one told us," Bob said.

"Of course I never told you," Sven said. "And God knows Lily would never tell you."

"Don't take the Lord's name in vain, Sven," Fanny told him. She winced at the look her brother gave her.

"Why wouldn't Lily have told anyone?" Vivian asked.

Sven looked at her. "Would you have told anyone if Bob had been your husband?"

"*Bob?*" she said, not understanding.

"Robert was her husband's name," Sven told her. "*Bob*."

"*You criticized Lily for his suicide?*" Richard asked, not getting it.

"*I criticized her husband for what he did, nephew*," Sven responded stiffly. He drew in a labored breath. "She didn't like that."

He tried to cleanse the moment by adding, in his usual jocular style, "Evelina is right. I *do* have trouble remaining quiet."

"But *why*, Uncle?" Bob continued. "What was there about…what Bob did that made you criticize him?"

"Let's not talk about it," Sven said.

"*Let's not*," Evelyn agreed.

Bob drew in a long breath. "Why did he do it, Uncle?" he went on.

Sven gave up trying to withhold the discussion. "His career was… foundering," he said.

"He was a photographer, wasn't he, Uncle?" Francis asked.

"A very successful one," Sven told them. "Then it all fell apart, I never heard why. All I knew was that he didn't get any work for months on end."

"He was very nice," Vivian said. She sounded sad.

"Yes, he was." It was as though Sven was trying to soften his criticism. "He was a good provider. A good husband. A good father. That's probably what made him lose heart when there was no work coming in."

"Was Lily understanding?" Richard asked.

"*What was there to understand?*" Sven demanded.

"Well…I can understand how he felt," Richard said.

"*And what he did?*" Sven kept demanding.

"*Yes,*" Richard answered. "That too."

"Well, *I don't,*" Sven snapped. Jocularity had vanished now. Every one seemed taken back by its abrupt departure. "I was a big success in Norway," he said. "Columbia was going to give me a recording contract."

Evelyn failed to get his point. "Are you sure?" she asked.

"*Yes,* Evelina," Sven said irritably. "I'm sure. But before I could sign the contract; brother Albert decided that we all had to go to the United States."

"Except for me," Fanny said.

"You were too young," Sven told her. "You had to go to a relatives. Gussie couldn't take care of you. She had Bill and Marie and Vera to raise."

"I went anyway," Fanny said.

"You went because you screamed and took on so that Albert didn't have the heart to leave you behind. Now will you let me finish?"

"Sorry," Fanny said. She wasn't.

"The point *is,*" Sven continued. "I was a success before we came to America. But did I let the blues get me? Did I kill myself? *No.* I borrowed enough money—from *Bert,* Fanny—from *Bert,* and bought a second-hand buffer so I could start a floor-polishing business. Do you think it was easy? To get started? It wasn't. It took me a year to find any regular work. Do you think I enjoyed that? *No, I didn't.* But I had a wife and two young sons. *Just like Bob had.* They were my responsibility. So I worked and supported them. I didn't put a shotgun barrel in my mouth and blow my head off! *Leaving it to my wife to clean it up in the morning!*" Sven's face was red now. He seemed to regret what he'd said.

Only Fanny responded. "Is it necessary to use language like that, Sven?" she said.

"No, I could *sing* it, Fanny," Sven responded. He improvised. "*I lost my job. I had a terrible feeling. So I blew my brains all over the ceiling.*"

"For pity's sake, Sven!" Fanny protested.

"Don't you mean for God's sake, *Fasa?*"

"I don't take the Lord's name in vain," Fanny told him.

"*No,*" Evelyn agreed. "Do you ever go to church at all, brother?"

"I go *every* Halloween," Sven answered. "Like clockwork."

"Very funny," Evelyn was frowning.

"Can we stop this talk now?" Fanny asked.

"*No,*" Vivian said.

"You heard it," Sven told his sister. "From the mouth of a babe."

"I'm not listening," Fanny said. Vivian's lips pressed together.

"I don't see how we can stop now," Bob began.

"Pandora's Box has been opened," Richard told his mother.

"*That's right,*" Francis broke in, sounding pleased. "I read about that a few days ago."

"Well, bully for you, Francisco," his sister said.

"Oh, *clam up,*" he told her, scowling.

"*You* clam up," she countered.

"*Children,*" Evelyn sounded tired. Vivian made a contemptuous sound. Francis kept scowling. "We're all sorry Lily couldn't make it to the service," Evelyn told Sven.

"She would have come if the service was for me," Sven told her.

"I don't believe that," Evelyn said.

"Evelina, you have a problem with reality," Sven was sharp with his sister. "You're unable to accept it."

"And *you are?*" she snapped back at him.

"*More than you,*" he snapped at her.

"*Children,*" Fanny said, trying to control the mounting conflict.

It was too late, Evelyn ignored her sister and kept attacking... "You were a star in Norway?" she challenged Sven. "You made one record that didn't sell. There was a contract with Columbia? No there wasn't."

"I *said*," Sven tried to suppress her.

"*Who are you to tell me I have a problem with reality?*" Evelyn cut him off.

"*Who am I?*" he demanded. "Who am I, Evelina?" he drew in a wheezing breath. "*I'm a brother who saw you marry beneath yourself!*" There was fury in his voice.

Several moments of heavy silence filled the table. Then Sven murmured, in Norwegian, "I'm sorry, sister. I didn't mean to say that."

"But you *did* say it," Evelyn said. "That's what you really think? *Beneath* myself? What was I?" She switched to Norwegian, "A beautiful debutante with a millionaire daddy living in an expensive mansion?"

Sven turned defensive. "Pop was an intellectual," he said in Norwegian.

"*Talk so we can understand you*," Vivian said irritably.

"Yes, Uncle," Bob agreed.

"I had no choice, Sven," Evelyn went on in English.

"No *choice*?" Sven saw an opening. "What are you, a troglodyte?"

Francis snickered, then realized it was out of place and became still again.

"I was an ugly duckling, brother," Evelyn said to him in Norwegian again.

"*What did she say?*" Vivian asked, very angry now.

"She said she was an ugly duckling," Gladys told her.

"Oh," Vivian said.

"It's not true," Fanny declared.

"You understand Norwegian?" Francis said to his cousin. Gladys didn't reply.

"Evelina, you were *cute!*" cried Sven.

"Thank you but I wasn't," Evelyn said quietly. She was hurt now. There was a glisten of tears in her eyes.

"*Oh, Evelina*," Sven said guiltily.

Evelyn was looking at her sister. "You know it's true, Fasa," she said. "*Fanny*, I mean!" She shook off Fanny's rejecting expression. "I had two gorgeous sisters."

"*No*," Fanny argued.

"*Yes*, Fasa," Evelyn said. "You know you were a beauty. So was Alicia." Her voice broke as she finished. "What wealthy, handsome devil was going to ask for my hand in matrimony?"

"Oh, stop it, sis," Sven said. "You were young, you were cute. You had a great figure." He waived away her gesture of denial. "*Yes, you did*," he said. "You rivaled Gladys."

Gladys drew back in surprise.

"That can't be news to you," Sven told her.

"Well…" Gladys didn't know what to say.

"Gladys knows what you're saying," Evelyn was dabbing at her eyes. "There she goes again," Vivian mumbled. "With two handsome brothers," Evelyn finished.

She realized immediately how Gladys reacted to her words and her eyes turned up again. "We're two of a kind," she said, realizing instantly that her added remark didn't help at all.

"*You were funny, too*," Sven told his sister abruptly. "You *were*. You made us all laugh."

"Ugly ducklings do that," Evelyn replied softly.

"Evelina, stop," Fanny urged.

"No, let her go on," Sven instructed. "Until she realizes that she could have had any one she wanted," he grimaced. "Instead, she married Tollet."

"He's a *good man*," Evelyn said, defensive now.

"Sure he's a good man," Sven backed off. "Who's denying it? The point is: *did he become anything?*"

"*He's a hell of a carpenter*," Francis told his uncle. He sounded resentful. He ignored the looks he got from his mother and aunt.

"*All right*," Sven said. He knew he was trapped but refused to surrender. "He's a—" He glanced at his sister Fanny, "—a *heck* of a good carpenter," he said. "Also a good *janitor*. Evelina, he did better in *Norway*. He was a first class blacksmith there."

"That's interesting," Richard said. "One day when I was helping him build that fence out front, I asked him if there was anything but carpentry he'd rather be doing and he said he'd like to be a blacksmith. I didn't know he'd been one in Norway."

"Sven, I think you aren't being fair to Evelina," Fanny said.

"I suppose not, Fanny, but she *did* have other suitors," he replied. "I never understood why she chose Tollef." His voice hardened. "Choosing not to face reality," he said.

"*At least he doesn't drink*," Evelyn said.

"Oh, *yeah?*" Francis said.

Evelyn looked startled. "What does *that* mean?" she asked worriedly.

"I'll tell you later," Francis said. Adding quickly, "When it's my turn."

"*My* turn," Vivian contradicted.

"What is it *with* you two?" Evelyn asked. "Your turn to do *what?*"

"Telling the *truth*," her daughter said.

"About *what?*" Evelyn asked. She was getting agitated now.

"You'll find out," Vivian told her.

"Find our *what*, sister?" Evelyn raised a dissuading hand. "I know, I know. You're not my sister. Never said you were."

"Then why do you—?" Vivian began.

"It was a *nickname*," her mother said. "Like *Fasa* for Tante Fanny. A *nickname*."

"*I don't like it*," Vivian said.

"Well, I'm *sorry*." Evelyn didn't sound it. She was angry now. She turned to her son. "*Tell me now*," she told him.

"What's happening to this party?" Fanny asked, distressed.

Vivian snorted. "*Party*," she said.

"You know what I meant," her aunt told her.

"People are speaking their minds, Mom," Bob told her. "That's what's happening."

"Well, I don't like it," Fanny said. "That's not why we're here."

"*Maybe it is*," Richard suggested.

That reduced everyone to silence. Broken by Bob who said, "Well, maybe it *is*. Who knows?" He added, "Maybe it's about time, too."

"*Right!*" Francis enthused. Again, his mother gave him a look.

"Maybe so," Sven said. "In which case—*Evelina*: I want you to divorce Tollef and run off with a Spanish Flamenco dancer."

"Find me one, brother," Evelyn said.

"All right, it's my turn now," Francis said.

"Oh, *go ahead*," Vivian grumped.

"I don't like that sound in your voice," Evelyn said to her son.

"You won't like what I have to say either," he responded.

"Oh dear—*Lord*." Evelyn was beside herself now.

"*Yippee*," Vivian said.

"I'm all ears," Sven added.

Fanny winced. "Is this really necessary, Francis?"

"Was it necessary for you to speak your mind, Tante?" he asked.

Fanny sighed, "All right."

"In keeping with speaking our minds," Sven said, "All this talk about Bert drinking…before anyone mentions *my* drinking, let *me* mention it. I was a drinker. I don't drink now. But I did once. A lot."

"*Is that why your wife left you*?" Vivian rushed in.

"My wife did not leave me, *child*," Sven declared stiffly. "We *separated*," he paused. "*Mutually*," he added.

"Sounds familiar," Vivian said.

"And what does *that* mean?" he demanded. There was ice in his voice.

"Oh, this is going too far," Evelyn said.

"Yes, it is," her sister agreed. She looked at her brother. "I think that was meant for me," she said.

"How so?" he asked, still aggravated.

"Bert and I *separated*, too. He didn't leave me."

"*No, he didn't*," Bob said.

His mother looked at him curiously.

"All right," Sven said. "If this is really truth telling time, here's mine. I treated my wife well. She deserted me anyway."

"*Why*?" Vivian kept at it. Her uncle gave her a critically questioning look. "My niece is really going for the throat today," he said. A minor laugh circled the table.

"We just want to know the truth, Uncle," Vivian told him. "We've heard stories for years."

"Didn't know I was the subject for discussion all these years," Sven said. There was no way of knowing if he was serious or not.

"You don't have to tell us, Uncle," Bob sympathized. "It's really none of our business."

"No, no," Sven said, half good-naturedly by now. He made a neighing sound. "Straight from the horse's mouth." A few of them smiled.

"Why did Ella leave me?" he continued. "I can't say I know. Was it my drinking? It didn't make that much of a problem. I never drank at home."

"Neither did Bert," Fanny said.

"Please, Fasa, let me confess," Sven rebutted. "I press on. Why did she leave? Allow me to shock you. Our...love life, our *romantic* life was good. No, it wasn't. She hated it."

"*Brother*," Evelyn appealed.

"No, she did," Sven went on as though his sister was only curious. "She liked having babies. She enjoyed carrying Eddie and Albert and Lily. It gave her an excuse not to endure romance for nine months, *ten*, with one of them, I forget which one."

"Brother, *don't*," Fanny pleaded now. "You don't have to—"

"Yes, I do!" Sven cut her off sharply. "Ella loved babies! She just didn't care for how we made them! There! *That's enough truth for you?*"

"Maybe more than we need, Uncle," Mary said quietly.

"Amen," Evelyn said.

"I'm not done yet," Sven continued stubbornly. "Was there another man?"

"*Sven*," Fanny begged. "*Enough.*"

"No, *not enough*," Vivian said.

"Sister, *hush-up*," her mother ordered. "All right, *not* sister...just *hush-up*."

"*No*," Vivian refused.

"Bravo," Sven said. "Let's not surrender now. *Was* there another man? There might have been. Ella was a beautiful woman."

"Yes, she was," Fanny broke in, trying to lighten the moment. And failing.

"She was very beautiful," Evelyn added hopefully.

"*Yes*," Sven agreed darkly. "She could have had her choice of men."
He stared at his sister. "Like *you*, Evelina!" he said.

"Oh, let's not go into that again," his sister begged.

"Why not?" Sven asked. "I thought this was truth telling time."

"It *is*," Francis broke it. "And it's *my turn*."

"Haven't we had enough?" Evelyn asked in a pained voice.

"*No, we haven't*," Vivian told her. "And I go after Franny."

"Good Lord," Evelyn muttered. "Some afternoon."

"Would you rather we stopped, Tante?" Bob asked.

"Yes, I would," Evelyn answered.

"*Amen*," Fanny said.

"*No*," Vivian declared.

"Oh, dear," Evelyn shook her head slowly.

"*Not until I've had my turn*," Vivian said.

"*And mine*," Francis added.

Evelyn sighed. "I give up," she said.

"*Good!*" Sven went on, "So did Ella. Choose another man instead
of me? Who knows? I suspected it for a long time. But I never knew for
sure. I still don't. So I live with it day by day. Was that what happened?
Or was it something else? All I know is I had three children to raise all
by myself."

He clapped his hands, startling everyone. "Take your choice, folks,"
he said.

They were all silent. Then Evelyn said, "I'm sorry, brother. I really
am."

"Thank you, Evelina," he smiled at her.

"I'm sorry, too, Sven," Fanny said. "I know what it's like raising
children alone."

"Necessary or not," Bob murmured. Only Mary heard him. She patted his leg.

"Thank *you*, Fanny," Sven said. "No, no. Frances."

"Thank you for telling us, Uncle," Bob told him. "Yes, thank you,"
Mary added.

Silence for a few moments. Then Sven said, "Your turn Francis.
Not you, Fanny. Nephew Francis." He looked at his nephew. "Take it
away, big boy," he said.

Evelyn spoke to her son. "Do you have to?" she asked, imploringly. She had dreaded this moment since Francis was born. She knew exactly what her son's "turn" entailed. So does Vivian. She was looking sternly at her brother. "*Go ahead*," she told him. It was less an encouragement than an order.

"I wish I had Uncle's sense of humor," Francis said.

"*Go ahead*," Vivian said. There was no doubt now. It was an order.

"I think I know what this is about," Sven said. "So do you, Evelina."

"Yes," she murmured. So softly, that no one heard her.

"So does Vivian," Sven said.

"I'm *waiting*," Vivian told everyone.

Everyone heard Evelyn's sigh of submission. Sven looked at her accusingly. "I told you it was the doctor, Evelina—*who delivered Francis*, his forceps work was too clumsy."

"*Uncle*," Mary broke in. "I know you've said this before—but it simply isn't true. It had nothing to do with a bungled forceps delivery. Francis has a cleft palate. An affliction that occurs during pregnancy."

"*No*," Sven insisted. "That isn't true. It happened because of the forceps delivery. It was *clumsy*."

"*Must* we?" Evelyn whispered.

"Francis has a *cleft palate*, Uncle," Mary told him. "No more, no less."

"Mary how can you—?"

"*She's right, Uncle Sven*," Francis interrupted. His uncle looked startled by the anger in his nephew's voice.

"It wasn't a clumsy forceps delivery," Francis said. "It's a cleft palate. I read about it. The delivery was not the crime." Everyone knew what he was going to say next. He said, "*The crime was doing nothing about it*."

He exhaled labouredly. "A crime I'm guilty of as much as—"

"Me, of course," Evelyn cut him off. She looked at her son with straining hope. "We took you to a practitioner."

"Tante, you should have taken him to a *doctor*!" Mary sounded close to anger.

"*I tried to be a good mother!*" Evelyn said, her voice cracking.

"And what did the practitioner tell you, Tante? Read the lesson twice a day? *Expect a quick healing?*" Richard was close to anger as well.

"Richard, *please*," his mother said.

"*I don't remember what he said*," Evelyn told Mary.

"Yes, you do!" Vivian suddenly raged. "He said, 'Take Franny to a doctor!'"

"I don't remember that!" her mother raged back.

"You mean you don't *want* to remember it!" Vivian cried.

"Sister, why would you say such a thing?" her mother tried to calm the waters. "He was a Christian Science Practitioner."

"Exactly," Fanny said.

"He was smart enough to know that Franny needed to see a doctor," Vivian said.

"*Exactly,*" Richard echoed his mother.

"Franny never had a problem when he was young," Evelyn said.

"Not at all," Fanny agreed.

"Until he reached puberty and only got *stared* at by girls?" Richard challenged.

"Dick, take it easy," Francis said. "You're being too hard on your mother."

"That's right," Fanny said. She smiled at her nephew.

"*It isn't true?*" Richard demanded.

"Tone it down, Dick," Bob said. "You're cutting too deep."

Richard was completely angry now. "I'm barely started, Robert!" he cried. "We've barely started! You know that! And you're a part of it!"

"Not you?" Bob countered.

"Of course me," Richard answered. "Probably all of us."

"The plot thickens," Sven said. He paused. "Or is it my stomach from eating all that World Famous Lemon Cake?"

"Uncle, please," Mary said.

"Sorry, niece-in-law," Sven apologized. He paused. "Once more into the breach, dear friends—and wounded relatives," he said. "Who's next? Vivian Nelson, I believe."

"Franny was going to come to California to stay with me after the surgery," Richard said.

"*Surgery?*" said Evelyn. "I never heard about that."

"We weren't going to tell you until it was done," Richard told her. "We were just going to tell you Franny was paying me a quick visit."

"Some visit," Vivian said.

"*Surgery*," Evelyn repeated. Not questioning now but criticizing.

"You should have told us," Bob said.

"I was going to tell you," Richard told his brother.

"How did it happen?" Bob asked.

"I found a Park Avenue surgeon who was willing to do it," Richard answered.

"*For a lot of money*," Francis said.

Richard flared, "*So what*?! It's your life, Fran!"

Francis looked doubtful.

"If it put you in debt for ten years, wouldn't it be worth it?" Richard asked him.

Francis gestured an '*I don't know*' reply. He said it then, " I don't know."

"*Sure you do*," Richard told him.

"We'd help too," Bob said.

"As much as possible," Mary said. She didn't sound sure of her words.

"If we could," Sven said nailing the coffin.

"We'd try," Gladys added.

"I wouldn't want any of you to do that," Francis said.

"You remember Beverly, Tante?" Richard asked his aunt.

"Yes," Evelyn said. Faintly.

"She was willing to marry Fran. *She said so*," Richard continued.

"*If I had the operation*," Francis said.

"What's so terrible about that?" Richard probed.

"For *seventy-five thousand dollars*?" Francis was hurting now.

Richard wouldn't let go. "*So what*?" he said loudly. "*Screw the amount*!"

"Richard," his mother murmured. Richard ignored her. "If it was seven *hundred* thousand, what's the difference?! *It's your life*, Francis!"

"I know," Francis muttered. His tone was dismal now.

"And no matter what any one says, don't you think we all would have helped you?" Richard demanded.

"I wouldn't ask that," Francis replied.

"We would have," Bob said.

"As much as we could," Mary added.

"*Sure*," Richard said. "Uncle Sven? Gladys?"

"Yes, of course," Sven said. Unconvincingly.

"We'd try to help," Gladys said. She sounded trapped.

"It would have added up," Mary said.

"Thank you," Francis said. "All of you. It's just..." he couldn't go on.

"You could stay in Los Angeles until you were healed," Richard told his cousin.

"And become a Hollywood Big Shot," Mary added.

"Oh, shut up," Richard told her good-naturedly. Everyone laughed.

Richard spoke seriously then. "You could do it, Fran," he said. "And when you came back it would be a new you."

"A new me," Francis said somberly.

"Yes, a new you," Richard said. "Completely different."

Francis was very still. Everyone looked at him in expectation. Finally, he spoke. "No," he said. "It's too late."

"It's *not*!" Richard exploded. "The surgeon doesn't think so!"

"He *does*," Francis said. "He said it should have been done when I was a baby."

"Well, it *should* have been," Richard conceded. "But it's not too late."

"Maybe it is," Mary said. Bob looked at her curiously.

"Good God, what does *that* mean?" Richard asked, beside himself with frustration.

"It means that Francis is so used to living the way he does, he can't imagine living any other way," Mary spoke without animosity, but with sympathetic understanding.

Richard sensed that she was right but was unwilling to give up the argument. "It would still be worth it," he insisted.

"You know what I'm saying," Mary said.

"Yes," Richard agreed. "I understand. But—"

"Well, *I don't*," Vivian broke in. She'd been listening to what everyone had said. Now she had to express herself. "Let me get this straight," she said. "*Beverly would only marry you if you had the operation?*"

"Is that so hard to understand?" Her brother asked.

"*Yes*. It *is*," Vivian objected.

"Vivian, it means that Beverly loves everything about Francis," Mary explained. "There's also the possibility that the one thing that may disturb her could be taken care of. What's so bad about that?"

"If she loves him, she should ignore the rest," Vivian persisted.

"Maybe the rest is something that *can't* be ignored," Francis snapped at her. "Can *you* ignore it? You've lived with it your whole life."

"We're not talking about me," Vivian mumbled.

Francis ignored her response. He turned to his mother. "What about you, Mom?" he asked. "Why didn't you have me fixed when I was born?"

"You said it yourself, darling," she told him. "The *cost*. The *cost*."

"Was it that much so long ago?" he asked.

"We simply couldn't afford it, dear," she said. "You know it was The Depression."

"Why didn't you ask Uncle Bert if you could borrow it?" Francis said. "He was doing pretty good, so I heard."

"We simply couldn't, Francis," his mother replied. "We tried never to borrow."

"*So you let me stay like this*," Francis said, completely angry.

"Darling, you're not being fair," his mother said.

"No, Francis, you're not," Fanny told him.

"*Mom, let him talk, will you?*" Gladys said irritably. Fanny looked at her daughter in surprise but said no more.

"It was all we could do, darling," Evelyn told her son.

"Do you know what it was like?" Francis asked. When his mother didn't reply, he added, "Mom, *do you have any idea at all what it was like for me?*"

"I think I do," Evelyn said softly.

"*Do* you, Mom?" Francis demanded. "Do you *really*?"

"Are you turning against me, son?" she asked.

"No, Mom! I'm not turning against you!" he cried. "I'm just trying to find out if you knew what it was like for me. If you *know* what it is like for me."

"I think I do," she said.

"Well, let me tell you in case you don't," he continued brokenly. "Can you even guess what it was like to be *stared* at all the time? Little kids are the worst. They have no shame. They stared at me as though I was a freak in the circus."

"*Son*," Evelyn pleaded.

"If they were with their parents, the parents would get a sad, polite smile on their faces and you know what they're thinking. *Thank God my kids don't look like that!*"

"Was it *that bad*?" his mother asked in a weak voice.

"Or *worse*," Francis told her. "Sometimes grown-ups look at me the same way. As if I was Lon Chaney in some horror movie. And *disgust*. I've seen that too."

Evelyn drew in a wavering breath. "I'm sorry," she murmured.

"*Sorry doesn't do it*, Mom," Francis told her angrily. "You should have had it fixed!"

"What about what Richard is saying?" Evelyn asked, surrendering now.

"It's too late, Mom!" Francis almost yelled. "God damn it to Hell, it's too late!"

"There's no need for cursing, son," Evelyn said. Vivian groaned and her mother looked at her coldly.

"It's *not* too late, Fran," Richard said in a calm voice.

"Oh, *please*," Francis responded to his cousin.

Dead silence filled the room. After some seconds had passed, Sven said, "I still say you should have sued that doctor."

"*No*, Uncle," Mary said.

"*You don't know*!" Sven raged unexpectedly.

Mary gave up. "You're right," she said. "I don't know."

"You could have had me operated on, Mom," Francis said. "You could have borrowed the money." He suddenly flared with anger again. "You could have robbed a bank for Christ's sake!" He scowled exaggeratedly. "For *goodness* sake," he corrected.

"As a matter of fact, your father was *planning* to rob a store," his mother told him.

Francis was moved by her words. "He *was*?" he asked meekly.

"Yes, he was," his mother replied. "I had to move heaven and earth to talk him out of it."

"Why *did* you?" Vivian wanted to know.

"Oh, for heaven's sake, sister! *I mean Vivian*! Would it have been better with your father in *prison*?!"

"Why prison, Evelina?" Sven said. He was serious. "I would have helped him. We could have gotten away with it."

"*Oh, Sven*," Evelyn's tone was defeated.

He seemed to know the absurdity of his suggestion. "Why not?" he said with a straight face. "Instead of Bonnie and Clyde, Tollef and Sven, The Terrible Norsky Two."

Evelyn groaned. There was limited laughter from everyone. The joke had not gone over too well.

"You really should think about it, Francis," Bob said.

Francis sighed. "Okay, Bob," he said. "Okay."

"So, Francis," Sven said. "Have you had your say?"

"I think so," Francis told him. He drew in a quick breath. "As long as my mother understands that I'll be alone for the rest of my life."

Evelyn's reply was hurt. "Your family doesn't count?" she asked.

"Are you guys going to live fifty more years, Mom?" Francis asked. "Is *Pop*? Am I supposed to live the rest of my life with Vivian?"

"*Thanks a lot*," his sister snarled.

"I mean what if you get married?" her brother said.

Now she *did* snarl. "*Fat chance*," she said.

"*Vivian*," her mother protested.

"Mom, *I'm* thirty-two years old," Francis said. "I'll never have a wife. Or a girlfriend. A *real* girlfriend. Sure, Beverly said she'd marry me — but only if my face is fixed."

"What about Mary Mulroy?" his mother suggested.

Francis' laugh was humorless. "A *Catholic*, Mom?" he said. "Are you kidding?"

Vivian made a sound of revulsion. "Good God," she muttered.

"What's wrong with a Catholic?" Mary asked.

"*Nothing*," Francis told her. "That's not what we're talking about."

"I hope not," Mary said.

Francis spoke to his mother again. "Anyway, Mary Mulroy doesn't like the way I look either," he said.

He cut off his mother's interruption. "I've seen it on her face, Mom!" he told her. "I'm an expert at that! I've seen the same look on faces all my life. They don't know I've seen it! They turn away but they have that look. Horror and disgust did I say? Mostly disgust. *Sickened disgust.*"

"Surely not," his mother said unhappily.

"Yes, Mom. *Surely*," Francis said.

"Oh, darling," Evelyn murmured. She attempted another possibility. "How about some nice Christian Science girl?"

"Sure, Mom," his rejoinder was flat. "She'd look at my face and tell me it was only a claim, I should read the lesson more often."

"What about Edna Wilson?" Evelyn said.

"Mom, she's *ugly*!" he cried. "She's a *hunchback*!"

"Beggars can't be choosers!" she said without thinking.

"Thanks, Mom," Francis said quietly. He sighed. "Case closed," he finished.

"Don't you think you're being a little harsh, Francis?" his Aunt Fanny said.

"The truth can be harsh, Tante," he replied.

"*That's* the truth," Sven said.

Francis looked at his aunt. "Still… I know you mean well, Tante," he told her. "But you can't understand what I'm talking about. You've always been beautiful."

Fanny was torn between pleasure at the compliment and a desire to be helpful to her nephew. "Well…" was all she could say.

"How old were you when Uncle Bert asked you to marry him?" Francis asked. "Eighteen?"

"Sixteen," she said.

"When I was sixteen, I couldn't even get a date. I was afraid to ask." He pulled in a labored breath. "I'm *still* afraid," he said. "I have friends, that's all." He turned to Gladys. "Bernie is my best friend," he told her. "He's been like a brother to me."

Gladys smiled. "He loves having you for a friend," she said.

"I'm glad," Francis answered.

"We'll, *somebody* has a friend anyway," Vivian's voice was sour.

"Oh, come on, Viv," Gladys protested.

"It's not like having a girl in my life," Francis said to his mother. "You understand that?"

"Yes," said Evelyn. "I do."

"I now declare you son and Mother who understands," Vivian announced.

Evelyn had difficulty reigning in her reaction. "You have something to say, sis?" she said.

"Yes. I have something to say!" Vivian reacted loudly. "I am not your goddam sister! Tante Fanny is! I'm your *daughter*! *Vivian*! Vivian Eleanor Nelson!"

"*I know that*, Vivian," said her mother, her anger barely contained.

"*Do* you, Mother? *Do* you really?" Vivian demanded.

"Guess it's her turn now," Sven said.

"*I guess it is*," Vivian snapped at her uncle.

Gladys sigh was audible to everyone. "What a lovely afternoon," she said. "I can't remember when I had such a good time."

"Said the lady with a husband and four children," Vivian said coldly.

"Oh, come *on*, Vivian," Gladys said. "I thought we were friends."

"*Think again*," Vivian said.

Gladys stood up. "I really should be leaving," she said. "Bernie's babysitting and he has to go—"

"*Don't go*, sis," Richard said.

"Why?" she asked. "So I can be attacked too?"

"We'll all have our turn," Richard told her.

"*Swell*," Gladys said crisply. "I can hardly wait."

"Me, too," Sven said. "Oh, no. I've already had my turn. I should go home. My dog is babysitting. No, he's not. There's no babies there. Well... I'll stay then. Don't want to miss the rest of this blood bath. Too exhilarating."

"*Are you done?*" Vivian asked him.

"Done and well done," her uncle said.

"Then I can speak," Vivian said.

"Yes, you can," Gladys said, frowning.

"*Thanks a million*," Vivian growled.

"Vivian, why are you so angry with me?" Gladys asked, honestly curious now. "I thought we were friends. *Really*. We've been to the mountains together. We've gone shopping together. Gone to the movies together. So why? *Why?*"

Vivian's anger became sullen. "Maybe I'm tired of being told how to live," she said.

"Do *I* tell you that?" Gladys wanted to know.

"Well..." Vivian had to accede.

"I think she meant me," Evelyn remarked.

"Say what you want to say, Vivian," Gladys told her.

Vivian hesitated, then she said, "It's a little hard with your mother glaring at you." She had lost the edge in her voice.

"Say what you have to say—*daughter*," Evelyn instructed.

Vivian looked chastened.

"*Vivian*," her mother reminded her.

Vivian stiffened. "All right," she said. "I *will*."

"Batten down the hatches," Sven said. No one smiled.

"Francis asked—if you understand that he'll be alone the rest of his life," Vivian said to her mother. "What do you think's going to happen to me?"

Evelyn's reply was taut. "You'll marry and have children," she said.

Vivian flashed at her. "*Come on!*" she said. "Marry and have children? *In what universe?!*"

"*It will happen*," her mother replied, stiffly.

"No, it won't!" Vivian cried. "Not for one second!" She waited for her mother's objection. When it didn't come, she added, "*Did it happen with Billy McAndrew?*"

Evelyn wouldn't yield. "You know why," she said.

"Sure I know!" Vivian had regained her fury. "Because he's *Catholic*! And we're Christian Scientists! And Catholics are walking in darkness! That's what you always say!"

"*Wait a minute*," Mary broke in.

Evelyn ignored her. "Well, they are," she said.

"So you chased him out of the house!" Vivian said.

"*I did not chase him out of the house*," her mother corrected, offended now.

"*Wait a minute*," Mary tried to break in.

Vivian was too enraged with her mother to allow Mary to continue. "You told him you couldn't consider having Catholic children in our house!" she yelled. "What was he supposed to do?! Hang around for ice cream and cookies?! You chased him out! He wanted to marry me and you chased him out!"

Evelyn's lips were pressed together. She had nothing more to say on the subject.

Mary was far from finished.

"Tante, we have six lovely girls. *All Catholic.* Are they all walking in darkness?"

Evelyn was unwilling to back down. "I hope not," she muttered.

"What the hell does that mean?" Mary challenged her. "That they *may* be 'walking in darkness'? For Christ's sake, Tante!"

"Take it easy, Mar," Bob tried to calm her down.

"Robert, you're their father! Doesn't it bother you at all what your aunt is saying?"

"*Yes*, Mar. It *does*," he said. "I just don't think it's the right time to discuss it."

"*Why not?*" Richard assailed his brother.

"Yes, *why not* ?" Mary echoed. "If not now, *when?*"

"Can't say I disagree," Sven said. He frowned at Evelyn. "You don't want Catholic children in your house? Why not? Do they have horns or something?"

"Bob is right," Evelyn said, struggling for control. "This isn't the right time to discuss it."

"I agree," Fanny said.

"Maybe we should leave," Mary said to her husband.

"No, you don't!" Vivian cried. "*Not now!*"

"I agree with that," Francis said to Fanny.

"So do I," Sven said. He winked at Bob. "We haven't gotten to you yet," he said, half seriously.

"I dread the moment," Bob said. He tried to say it lightly but failed.

"I haven't been on the grill yet either," Richard said.

"How comforting," Bob said, meaning otherwise. Richard grinned, misunderstanding.

"I think I've heard enough," Evelyn said. "We went to a *funeral* today. This conversation is hardly appropriate."

"My life has *never* been appropriate," Vivian further dampened the moment.

"Can we talk about it later?" Evelyn asked.

"*No!*" Vivian cried grimly. "*Now or never.*" She glared at her mother. "I could have been married!" she said.

Her mother's voice grew cold. "It would have been a mistake."

"Win a husband, lose a mom," Sven said. Evelyn gave him a teeth-clenched look.

"*I could have been married,*" Vivian repeated insistently. "Instead of being a fat, old maid."

"This is a terrible conversation," Fanny said, disturbed.

"I find it most illuminating," Sven said. Bob and Richard smiled. Francis looked angrily justified.

"You are not a fat, old maid," Evelyn told her. "You're not even thirty yet. You're an attractive young woman who hasn't met the right man yet."

"And never will," Vivian said. "Unless he's an ugly, hunchback Christian Scientist."

Everyone but the two aunts laughed. They both looked offended.

Evelyn's voice became imploring. "All I wanted was a happy household."

"How? By keeping it free of Catholics?" Mary asked.

Evelyn sighed heavily. "Am I such a terrible person?" she asked.

"Misguided," Mary told her.

"*All I wanted was a happy household*," Evelyn protested.

"Tante, you can't just *want* a happy household, you have to *make* it happy," Bob said.

"I *tried!*" Evelyn told him.

"Maybe what you wanted was a *controlled* household, Tante," Bob said.

"*Bingo*," Sven joined him.

"I guess I've just been wrong all my life," Evelyn's voice broke in self-pity.

"*No*," Fanny defended her sister.

"Not wrong, Evelina," Sven told her. "Maybe just trying too hard to keep things in order. To make them perfect."

"Not perfect," she said. "Just happy."

"And are you happy now?" Sven asked her.

"I'm *miserable*," she answered.

"Well, there you go," Sven said. "Happiness is not so easy to find."

"It sure isn't," Evelyn started to cry.

"Especially when you deal with the truth," Richard said.

"Oh, this has done me a lot of good!" Vivian lurched to her feet. "A *lot* of good!" she turned toward the parlor.

"Sis!" her mother cried. Adding in a guilty rage, "*Vivian!*"

"Let her go," Mary said.

Fanny tried to settle the tension. "Vivian, you're a very pretty girl!" she said loudly.

Vivian whirled, crying now. "No, I'm not!" she cried bitterly. "Bob is handsome! Richard is handsome! Gladys is—*they're all better looking than me!*"

"Thanks a lot, Vivian," Gladys said resentfully. "I appreciate the commendation."

"If I knew what that meant, I'd answer you!" Vivian said, still crying.

She lunged into the parlor crying out as she almost collided with her father. "*Hey!*" Tollef said.

Tollef Nelson was sixty-one years old, five-foot nine inches tall, weighing 160 pounds. He was not attractive but had a kind face and, when he was amused, a droll smile. He held on to his daughter concerned by her tears. "What's wrong?" he asked.

"We'll explain later," his wife said. Brushing at her own tears, she rose to greet her husband.

Fanny, who had gotten up to comfort her sister, sat back down.

"*Please*, Pop," Vivian said, sobbing. She pulled away from him and ran toward the front hall.

"What's going on?" Tollef inquired. He still wore his overcoat and hat; both were spotted by rain.

"Well, that's quite a story, Tollef," Sven told him. "We've been having a truth-telling orgy."

"An *orgy*?" asked Tollef. He took off his hat.

"Never mind," Evelyn told him. "I'll explain it all later." She started helping him remove his topcoat. "Raining," she said.

"Yes," he said. "What's wrong with sister?"

"We'll talk about it later," Evelyn told him. "Cleaning go okay?"

He nodded, still curious. "Why is sister crying?" he asked. "Good afternoon, Fanny and Gladys, Bob, Mary, Sven, Richard, Francis," he greeted them quickly.

"Don't call her sister, Pop," Francis told him. "She doesn't like it."

Tollef was even more confused by that. He was going to pursue it, then changed his mind. "What have I been missing?" he asked.

"Oodles," Sven said.

"Quite a bit, Uncle," Bob told him.

"*Truth telling*?" Tollef asked. His face was a mask of perplexity.

"At least," Sven said. "Pull up a chair, old man."

"Yes, sit down," his wife led him to his recliner chair by the window. "Are you hungry, darling? I'll fix you a plate."

Tollef exhaled an "*I wish I knew what was going on*" breath. He sat. "Too bad I wasn't here all along," he said.

"Too bad indeed," Sven said. "You missed the fireworks."

"Oh, dear," Tollef said. "I don't know what to ask first."

"Don't ask anything," his wife said in Norwegian. "Especially your brother-in-law. He's being silly."

"As usual," Tollef responded in Norwegian, a droll smile on his lips. "Shouldn't you go up and see if sister is all right?" he added in English, "Seriously."

"She'll be all right," Evelyn said. "Let her cry it out."

"Maybe not," Francis said.

"Never you mind," his mother told him.

"*As usual*," Francis said. He knew enough to say it in Norwegian.

Sven snickered at his nephew's accent. His mother gave him a critical look.

Upstairs, Vivian's bedroom door slammed.

"You missed quite a show, Uncle," Bob said.

"A *show*?" Tollef said. "An orgy?"

"An event," Bob tried to explain.

"A *cataclysm*," Sven said.

"Are you hungry, dear?" Evelyn asked, covering a plate with food.

"I could eat," Tollef answered. He looked at his brother-in-law. "So what was the cataclysm?"

"Not now, Tollef," his wife said. "Have something to eat first."

"That bad," Tollef said. It was uncertain if his smile was droll or concerned.

"Not *bad*," Evelyn tried to get out of the moment. "Just…"

"Bad," Sven finished.

"Yes, *bad*," Francis emphasized. His father looked at him curiously. "How did it happen?" he asked.

"Like I said," Sven told him. "Truth telling."

"Sven, *that's enough*." Evelyn abjured her brother.

"About *what*?" Tollef persisted.

"The family peccadilloes," Sven tried to explain.

"I don't know that word," Tollef said.

"The family mistakes," Sven said.

Tollef thought about it for a few moments; then sighed. "I should have just kept on cleaning toilets," he decided. Everyone laughed. Even Francis, who was not in a particularly good mood.

"So what are the mistakes?" Tollef asked.

"Can we talk about it later?" Evelyn said.

"*Evelina*," her brother cautioned.

She tightened. "*Later*," she said.

"*Now*," Francis said determinedly.

His mother groaned. "I just can't win," she said.

"Nobody wins this game, sis," Sven told her. There was no humor in his voice now.

"Nobody loses either, Tante," Bob said. "We all gain."

"*Do* we?" Mary said.

"Hopefully," Gladys said at the same moment.

"This sounds very serious," Tollef said.

"It *is*, Pop," Francis told him.

"What made it happen?" Tollef asked.

No one had an answer.

"What made it *start*?" Tollef asked.

"Probably a discussion of Bertolf's drinking," Sven told him.

Tollef blew out a gust of air. "After his *funeral*?" he questioned. Sven shrugged, without an answer. "Not so good," Tollef said.

"Not so good at all," Fanny said.

Tollef looked at her as though expecting an explanation. When she didn't provide one, Bob said—"Some of us blamed Mom for Pop drinking too much."

"That doesn't sound right," Tollef said.

"*No, it doesn't*," Fanny agreed, tensely.

Smiling in satisfaction, Evelyn handed Tollef the plate of food—a turkey sandwich, potato salad and cole slaw, and a slice of lemon cake. Francis brought coffee in his fathers' personal, over-size cup. Tollef thanked them in Norwegian. "You're welcome, my darling," Evelyn said, also in Norwegian.

Tollef took a bite of the sandwich. "*So*," he said. "You blame Fanny for Bertolf's drinking too much?"

"They *do*," Fanny said.

"Well, not exactly, Mom," Bob responded. "I just saw Pop's drinking get worse after you put him out of the house."

"I did not—!" Fanny cried. She broke off in disgust. "Oh, never mind," she said.

"I don't know how bad Bertolf's drinking got after he left Allendale," Tollef said.

"Bad enough to kill him, Uncle," Bob said.

"*Oh, for God's sake!*" Fanny unexpectedly raged.

"Watch it, Fanny," Sven warned, trying not to smile. "Mary Baker may have her eye on you."

"*I don't appreciate that, Sven,*" his sister told him.

"Never meant to be appreciated," Sven reacted. "Fanny. Frances. Fasa."

"What's going on here?" Tollef asked. "A Civil War?"

"At least," Sven answered.

"I told you we should talk about it later," Evelyn told her husband.

"No," he responded calmly. "It's interesting. We never talked about these things before." His lips tightened at his wife's expression. "Bertolf's drinking? Fanny putting him out of the house? That's it?"

"Not by half," Sven told him. "For instance, you saw how upset your daughter is."

"Yes, I want to find out about that," Tollef said.

"You will," Sven promised. "You'll get the entire picture. Including your son's part in it."

"And your brother-in-law," Francis informed his father.

"Right," said Sven. "And me."

"When we were talking about Bert's—*and Sven's*—drinking, I told everyone how glad I am that *you* don't drink," Evelyn said.

"And I said oh, *yeah?*" Francis said.

"That's right. He said that," Evelyn told her husband. "What did he mean?"

Tollef hesitated, giving his son an accusing look.

"Well, it *happened*," Francis defended himself.

"I guess it did," Tollef said to his wife. "He saw me in *Mario's.*"

"*Mario's?*" Evelyn said, suspiciously.

"A bar," he answered.

"*Oh, no,*" his wife's voice became plaintive. "A *saloon?*"

"Yes, Evelina," he said. "These things happen."

His wife was stricken. "Not in my life," she said.

"In *anybody's* life," he told her.

"What does it *mean?*" she said, begging now.

"It means that Francis caught me in *Mario's* having a beer," her husband said.

"A *beer*," she said. From the tone of her voice, it seemed more than she could deal with.

"Or two," Tollef said. His wife groaned softly. "Come on, Evelina," he said. "I'm not a drinker. I do it to relax after working all day. Is that so bad?"

"*Alcohol*," Evelyn sounded repelled.

"A little," Tollef agreed.

Evelyn changed gears abruptly. "Why was Francis there?" she asked.

"*For a drink*, Mom," Francis told her. "Not beer either. *Whiskey*. I *like* whiskey. *Wilson's*."

"Oh, God," Evelyn's world was crumbling.

"I don't think he'd mind," Francis quipped. "Do *you*, Pop?"

"Not sure I know the man," Tollef replied. Only Sven laughed at that.

"Sure," Evelyn said bitterly. "Make jokes about God. That's just perfect."

"I don't think Tollef was joking," Fanny tried, again, to ease the moment.

"This is getting very interesting," Sven said. "Beats lemon cake by a mile."

"That's for sure," Gladys said glumly.

"What about you?" Sven asked her. "No confessions to make? No one to attack?"

"I really have to go, Uncle," she told him. "My husband—"

"Gladys, *stay*," Richard interrupted.

"*Why?*" she wanted to know. "Why should I stay?"

"You'll see," he answered.

"Oh, boy," she muttered grimly. "More mystery."

Her voice suddenly broke. "*Haven't we had enough of that already?*"

"*Yes*," her mother concurred.

"Not mystery," Richard told his sister. "More like revelation."

Gladys released a long sigh. "I think Pop's the only lucky one in the family right now," she said. "He doesn't have to listen to any of this."

Richard, Bob and Mary smiled. Fanny and Evelyn didn't. Sven and Francis had no expression. Tollef looked confused again. "How could he?" he murmured. No one heard.

"So who's next on the burner?" Sven asked.

"Sven, for goodness sake," Fanny said.

"I repeat," Sven insisted. "Who's next on stage in The Funeral Follies?"

"You mean *post*-funeral, don't you, Uncle?" Francis corrected.

"I mean *post*-funeral, as you say, nephew," Sven agreed testily. "All right, who's next?"

"Bother Bob, I think," Richard said.

"Not you?" Bob shot back.

"I'm last," Richard told him. "Mine's probably the worst."

"Oh, my God," Fanny said, dispirited.

"*Mary Baker Eddy*," Sven reminded her.

"Oh, shut up," his sister said. Sven giggled. That was pleasantly unexpected.

"All right Robert Christian Matheson, prepare yourself," Richard told his brother.

"Maybe I'll just go home," Bob said.

"Not so," Sven informed him. "Not before we see you jeopardized."

"See him what?" Tollef asked.

"*Placed in danger*, Tollef," Sven said melodramatically.

"Oh, is that all?" Tollef remarked.

General amusement at that. Even from Bob who wasn't sure what was coming. Though he had a pretty good idea what it would be.

"Hasn't everyone been placed in that this afternoon?" Tollef said more than asked.

"Not you, Tollef," Sven told him. "You're beyond reproach."

"*Word*?" Tollef questioned.

"Means you are beyond all danger," Sven answered him. "Except, of course, at *Mario's*. We don't know what high jinks you've been involved in there."

Tollef laughed broadly.

"And unless you'd rather we went after you as well," Sven suggested. "We're getting pretty good at it."

"I'd rather go back to the toilets," Tollef said. Everyone laughed freely.

"Certainly less threatening," Sven said. Less laughter on that one.

"No one's going to go after you, darling," Evelyn told her husband. "*No one.*"

"Probably true," Sven said. "You're the only innocent one here."

"*Oh, yeah?*" Francis said.

"Nephew, please," Sven sighed. "You've already had your turn."

"So Pop is absolved just like that?" Francis queried.

Sven sighed. "Maybe later," he said.

"Absolved?" Tollef asked.

"*We'll talk about it later*," Evelyn said almost threateningly. Tollef gestured in surrender.

"Brother Bob, then," Sven said.

"*This whole thing stinks*," Mary sounded angry.

"I agree," Fanny said.

"Oh, let it go," Bob said. "We all know what it's going to be about anyway."

"Do we?" Gladys offered.

Her brother looked at her questioningly; then went on. "My position in The Matheson Drinking Clan," he said. "Allow me to present my case. As far as I'm concerned, unlike the other members of my family, I am *not* an alcoholic."

"Oh, come on," Francis objected. Fanny started to speak, then changed her mind.

"I'm *not*," Bob said. "I work too hard for too many hours and I get stressed out. I need to get away."

"On a binge," Francis said.

"Call it what you like," Bob told him. "To me, it's just an escape."

"*During which you're on a binge*," Francis insisted.

"You're really out to get me, aren't you?" Bob said. "What are you doing, looking for a drinking buddy?" Immediate guilt afflicted him. "I'm sorry," he said. "I didn't mean that."

"Or maybe you did," Francis reacted.

"Is Francis wrong, Bob?" Richard probed.

"All right," Bob replied. "I drink."

"In Hawaii," Francis said. "In Florida. In Tahiti."

"To *relax*, Francis," Bob told him. "To get rid of stress."

"Good explanation," Francis said. "That's why *I* drink too!"

"Francis, *does Bob drink when he's home?*" Mary said sharply. "*No. He doesn't.*"

"Except for gallons of Pepsi-Cola," Francis fired back her irritation.

"Getting sugar that way," Richard pointed out.

"*Exactly*," Francis agreed with his cousin. "Getting his sugar that way."

"You two are being very cruel," Mary told them.

"I *drink* to have something to drink," Bob explained. "By the way, can I get another bottle?"

Laughter at his request was tentative.

Francis stood up. "No, no, I'm just kidding," Bob told him. Grinning, Francis sat back down.

"Also, by the way," Gladys said to Mary. "About these so-called escapes. Why do you always see to it that Bob gets driven to the airport? Doesn't it ever occur to you to face his stress at home?"

"I give him what he needs," Mary told her coldly.

"And are your daughters going to drive him to the airport when they're old enough?" Gladys asked, also coldly.

"Gladys, calm down," Bob told her. "Mary only drives me when she can."

"When she *can*?" Gladys seethed. "When she's not too *busy* otherwise?"

"Here we go," Mary mumbled.

"She has the office to look after," Bob said. "She has the girls to look after."

"That's what this is all about, isn't it?!" Mary flared. "You don't have a Nanny!"

"I have my mother!" Gladys flared back.

"Does she *live* with you?" Mary demanded. "Do *everything* for you?"

"*That's the whole point!*" Gladys ranted. "You do *nothing*! Nanny does it all! Cooking and cleaning and laundry and taking care of the girls! That poor old woman with a million wrinkles on her face does *everything*!"

"And it pisses you off! *Doesn't* it?" Mary almost yelled.

"Yes, it pisses me off!" Gladys answered. "Because I do *everything*!"

"Oh, now, Gladys," Fanny objected.

"Well, it's true, Mom! You know it!" Gladys refused her mother's objection.

"Not *everything*," Fanny continued to object.

"Street language, girls," Sven said to Mary and Gladys.

"*Oh*... fuck off, Uncle!" Mary snarled.

"*Oh*, dear," Sven said.

"I'm sorry, Tante," Mary said. "I'm just fed up with attacks on my mother. Has anyone ever spoken to her? Has she complained about her life?"

"She wouldn't," Gladys said. "She's too kind."

"*Thank* you for saying something positive about her," Mary said.

"I haven't attacked *her*," Gladys returned.

"So I noticed," Mary said.

"Unlike your opinion of our mom," Gladys returned again.

"Which *means*?" Mary's cheeks began reddening.

"*Queen Bee*," Gladys reminded her.

Mary looked embarrassed. "Oh... well," she muttered.

"Yes or no?" Gladys challenged.

"It doesn't mean anything," Mary defended.

"It means you looking down your nose at her," Gladys said. "Just because she dresses well."

"And *never* does what Nanny does," Mary told her.

"I did all that and raised three children!" Fanny said angrily. "Am I supposed to feel guilty for wanting to take it easier now?"

"No, of course not," Mary assured her. "You're entitled."

"*But not me*," Gladys said. "Not *us*."

"*Us?*" Mary asked.

"Bernie works two jobs to keep us going," Gladys told her. "You have a lot more money than we do."

"Is *that* what this is all about?" Mary said.

Gladys ignored her. "Every time you've been to our house—a *much* less expensive one than yours—it was 'oh, you have a new refrigerator, I wish we had one.' Or— 'oh, a new dishwasher, we could really *use* one'."

"Sorry, I thought I was complimenting you," Mary said.

"Well, you weren't," Gladys replied. "You were reminding us that despite all your money, you were jealous of us."

"Sorry, Gladys," Mary said stiffly. "Stupid of me."

"Come on, girls. Let's not haggle," Bob told them. He looked around the table. "Everyone through attacking me?" he inquired.

"Pretty much," Richard told him. "Although I think you know that very few of us buy your 'I was only trying to escape' story. We think there's more involved. We think you're an alcoholic and won't admit it."

"*You* do anyway," his brother said. Not angrily but as a matter of fact.

"Why do you take this?" Mary stabbed at her husband.

"He takes it because he knows it's true," Richard told her. He cut off his brother's interruption. "I'm sure you don't remember when we picked you up at LAX, after your last binge."

At that word, Bob stiffened with anger.

Again, Richard cut off his brother's response. "You asked us to take you to a bar near the airport," he said. "So you could have a screwdriver. And, while we were there, you told me you could 'write me under the table' if you wanted to." He waited a moment, then added, "There's a whole world of meaning there, Bob."

"I don't remember that," Bob said.

"I told you I was sure you wouldn't," his brother replied.

Mary spoke to Richard now. "Bob said he knew his father's drinking got worse because his heart was broken when he couldn't live with his family anymore."

"Yes?" said Richard. "So?" He had no idea where this was going.

"Well, you broke your brother's heart when he asked you to become his partner and you refused him."

"Mar, please," Bob said.

"*No*," she resisted. "I'm glad I said it." She supressed a sarcastic smile. "It's that kind of afternoon, isn't it?"

"How true," Sven said. He raised a surrendering hand to Mary. "Okay, I'll fuck off."

"*Sven*," Evelyn pleaded.

"No, that's me," he said. "The family fuck-up."

Evelyn gave her husband a dark look as he laughed. Francis snickered quietly.

"I give up," Evelyn said.

"Just as well," her brother told her.

"I'm sorry you decided not to go into business with me," Bob told his brother. "I think it would have gone very well. But *broken my heart?*"

"Yes, *broken your heart!*" Mary plunged on. "You know it's true! You *told* me so!"

"Maybe I was drinking," Bob said half-seriously.

"*No, you weren't drinking*," Mary was angry with her husband now. "You told me you made up your mind to stop drinking so your brother would go into business with you."

"Maybe I would have," Bob said sadly.

"Maybe I would have," Richard echoed; equally sad. "No, that isn't true."

"It's *not?*" his brother asked in surprise.

"Oh, maybe partly," Richard said. "But mostly because of my writing."

"Some excuse," Mary mocked him.

"I know you think I haven't written anything worth a damn," Richard conceded.

"Not true," Bob said.

"Thank you, brother," Richard said. "I *will* write something worth a damn eventually."

"I know you will," Bob reassured him.

"Language, Richard," his mother prodded.

"Oh, for God's sake, Mom," Richard said, irritably. "All these things being talked about and you're still worried about language?"

"Yes. I am," she said.

"Something worth a *darn*, then. A *darn*." he amended.

"I know you will, too," she replied.

"*The Matheson Brothers*. That's all Daddy wanted," Mary said to Richard.

"Daddy?" Richard asked.

"Skip it," Mary said. "It's what we call him. He wanted very much for you to become his partner. He was *counting* on it—though God knows why. When you turned him down—" she overran Bob's attempt to speak. "I'm sorry but it's true!" she stormed. "*He broke your heart!*"

Richard exhaled forcibly. "I didn't know it was that important to you," he said to his brother.

"*You didn't break my heart*," Bob sounded aggravated. "Not you anyway," he added impulsively.

"Oh?" Richard said. "Who did then?"

"Never mind," Bob told him, already sorry for his impulsive remark.

"No, *don't* let it go," Mary said. "It's me, isn't it?"

"*Let it go*," Bob ordered her.

"*No*. It's me, isn't it?" Mary insisted. "*Isn't it?*"

"Must we go on like this?" Fanny asked.

Mary paid no attention to her. "*Isn't it*?!" she almost shouted.

Bob answered quietly. "Yes," he said.

"Round fifteen," Sven muttered. "*Bong*."

"All right Daddy-O," Mary challenged. "Let's have it." From the way she said it, it seemed clear that she knew what her husband was talking about.

"No," said Bob. "I'd rather not."

"Round fifteen cancelled," Sven said. Everyone looked at him warily. "Sorry," he mumbled.

act three

"No more," Bob said. "We've had enough recriminations."

"*Recriminations*," Mary snapped. "Oh, that sounds great."

Bob changed the subject deliberately. "Tante, does Vivian always stay in her room like this?" he asked.

"Not that much," Evelyn told him. At the same instant Francis said, "*Yes*. She stays there a lot."

"I can't win," Evelyn gave up.

"Evelina, no one wins," Sven told her. "This isn't a contest."

"Isn't it?" she denied.

Bob wouldn't give up. "What does she do in her room?" he asked.

Evelyn cut off Francis' answer. "Read or listen to the radio."

"Or *cries*," Francis said.

"Francis, *stop it!*" his mother demanded.

"She *cries*," Francis persisted. "I *hear* it! My room is right *next* to hers!"

"*That isn't all she does*," his mother fought back.

"It's all I hear!" he raged. "There's something *wrong* with her!"

"*No!*" Evelyn cried.

"*Yes!*" he cried back. "Why do you keep *denying*, Mom?! There's nothing wrong with me! Now there's nothing wrong with Viv! When will you admit there's something wrong with *both* of us! Pop won't say anything!"

"Now, wait," Tollef protested weakly.

"Well, it's true, Pop," Francis said. "Mom runs the show. You know that."

Evelyn dabbed at her eyes. "Oh, Francis, Francis," she murmured sadly.

"Well…" Francis was obviously retreating. "I just know—" he couldn't finish. Words eluded him.

Mary broke the heavy silence. "*Well*, Daddy?" she asked, her voice laden with ice.

"Well, I'm not going to say it," Bob told her.

"*Yes-you-are!*" she declared. Then, "It's that kind of fucking afternoon."

"*Mary*," Evelyn appealed softly.

"I'm sorry, Tante," Mary said. "But I have to know. It's important to me." She looked at Bob accusingly. "So… Robert Christian," she said. "You gonna chicken out?"

Bob tightened. His expression conveying, '*Not now I won't.*'

"You remember when they wanted me to be a member of the City Council?" he reminded her.

"I remember you turned them down," she answered. "Because you were afraid you'd show up at a meeting drunk."

"That's what I told you," he said. "That wasn't it at all."

"*What was it then?*" she asked coldly.

"*I was afraid my wife would offend them*," he answered.

Mary was clearly hurt but defensive. "I never heard *that* before," she argued.

"You never heard it because I never told you," Bob replied.

"Well, thanks for nothing," Mary said.

"You insisted on knowing. Now you know," Bob told her.

He turned nasty with sudden resentment. "You just didn't have the *class* to be a City Councilman's wife. I knew it would offend them."

Tears were welling now. "Great," Mary said. "Just great."

Bob already felt guilt. "I didn't *want* to tell you," he tried to explain. "True or false?"

Mary was sobbing now. "Oh, go to hell," she muttered.

"Oh, *Mar*," he said. Now he was in deep regret. He tried to take her hand but she pulled away. "*No*," she said, beginning to cry.

"Why did you insist on knowing? I would have been glad it remained a secret," he told her.

"Some secret," she almost sobbed the words.

"Do you prefer this?" he asked.

"I prefer we never came here at all," she told him.

"Maybe you're not the only one," Sven said. There was no humor left in his voice.

Gladys stood, "I'm going home," she said.

"*Not yet*," Richard told her.

"*God damn it!*" she said. Fanny winced but remained silent.

"Oh, we are really into naughty language now," Sven said. Unserious again.

"*Good*," Francis reacted. "A lot of things needed to be said."

"*Yes*," Richard agreed.

"Some weren't needed," Mary said.

"I'm sorry, Mar," Bob told her. "I never wanted to hurt you. But you kept insisting."

"I wouldn't have liked it any better knowing there was a secret being kept from me," Mary responded. "But then what do I know? I ain't got no class."

A laugh of genuine appreciation rounded the table.

"Please," Bob asked his wife. "Forgive me."

"That *would* be a classy thing to do," she said. "If I had any class."

More general laughter. Less certain now.

Smiling sadly, Bob put his arms around Mary.

She punched him on the arm. "*Ow!*" he said. Then, "Okay, I deserved that."

"Wait'll you see what happens when we get home," Mary told him. More general laughter. Genuine enjoyment once more.

"This has been some day," Evelyn said.

"It ain't over yet," Richard told her.

"Oy," Sven said. More tension releasing laughter.

Richard was half serious, half joking when he asked, "Gladys, does Bernie drink?"

Her groan was so obviously pathetic that it made everyone laugh.

"I take that for a no," Richard said. "Or yes."

"*No!*" her tone had become one of vehement amusement.

The laughter increased.

"He's not Norwegian anyway," Sven said. "German's don't count."

"I'm Norwegian and I don't drink," Tollef broke in. "Not too much anyway."

"Hey, everybody!" Evelyn shouted abruptly. "Who wants some booze?"

"Sis, sis, sis," Fanny smiled sadly.

"Let me say one more thing before this charming afternoon draws to a close," Bob said.

Vivian walked in quietly.

"*There she is!*" Sven sang. "*Miss America!*"

Vivian was not amused. The only one who was—vaguely—was Mary.

"Welcome back, Vivian!" Bob told her. "You've missed some goodies but you're just in time for my final declaration."

"Go ahead," she said. "I've already made mine."

"Oh, Viv," her mother's tone was disconsolate.

"Call me sis if you want," Vivian told her. Sporadic laughter greeted her remark. As Vivian sat down, her mother reached out to stroke her shoulders.

"Resolution," Sven said. "In the Nelson Family anyway."

"Not quite," Francis told him.

"You're right," his uncle concurred. "Not quite."

Silence for a few moments. Then Bob said, "Okay. My final declaration."

"Of Independence?" Sven asked.

"Possibly," Bob answered. He paused; then said, "I'll make the statement once more and that's *it*. I'm not an alcoholic," he overrode Richard's objection. "All right, I *believe* I'm not an alcoholic. Obviously, I can't prove it, so you'll just have to take my word for it. I work hard for too many days, hours. *That's* my problem. Once in a while, I *snap* and have to get away. What were referred to as my 'escapes.' Yes, I drink during those getaways. It relaxes me. I wish I didn't have to drink but I do. Then I come home, after a week, two weeks."

"A month," Richard said.

"Okay, a month," Bob conceded. "But then I come home and *stop* drinking. *Completely*. If I was an alcoholic, could I *do* that? Could I just stop drinking when I got home and start working again?"

"Overworking," Richard said.

"Okay. Overworking again," Bob agreed.

"Laying the groundwork for your next 'escape'?" Richard told him.

"Drinking gallons of Pepsi Cola," Francis added.

"Which is better than the hard stuff," Bob replied. He looked around the table. "So have I made my point? Could I function this way if I was an alcoholic?"

"Well, you do," Richard said.

"*Stop drinking and go back to work?*" Bob insisted.

"Until you snap again," Richard said.

Bob chose not to argue the point. "Until I snap again," he yielded. Picking up the Pepsi Cola bottle, he raised it in a toast. "Cheers," he said.

"All right," Richard went on. "Let's not belabor the point." He smiled. "I have something to say before I make my declaration."

"*Say* it then," Sven said with mock exasperation. "Let's put an end to all these damned declarations."

"What I have to say is not a complaint," Richard told him.

"Is that all you thought I was doing?" Vivian said. "*Complaining?*"

"And *me?*" Francis challenged.

"With justification," Richard said. "Both of you."

"With *what?*" Vivian asked.

"With good reason," Richard told her.

"Which leaves me out in the cold," Evelyn said in a subdued tone.

"Not at all, Tante," Richard said to her. "You did what you thought was right."

"Thanks," she responded. There was little gratitude in her voice.

"Richard's right," Bob said. "You're all good people. But we're all human and make mistakes. What Uncle Sven called *peccadilloes*. None of it was mean-spirited. Misguided maybe; but human. Honest mistakes."

"What I have to say is no mistake," Richard said. "It's pure praise for my brother."

Bob looked surprised. "I'm overwhelmed."

"You should be," Richard told him. "But I don't think you know how to be." He gazed at his brother admiringly. "Do you have any idea what you've accomplished, Robert?" he asked.

"A good deal of angst," Bob said.

"I don't mean today," Richard told him. "I mean in the last decade. The last twenty years."

"Tell me," Bob said with a half smile.

"*You created an empire*," Richard told him.

Bob looked incredulous. "An *empire*?"

Richard grinned. "All right, a *modest* empire. You haven't conquered any countries. You *have* conquered a world of business though. You did it as completely as you put together your stamp collection which could have made you rich if you'd sold it for what it was really worth."

"Don't remind him," Mary said. "Don't remind *me*."

Everyone laughed.

"Look at what you've done, Bob," Richard said. "You started out working in a Manhattan printing plant. Then you had your own printing plant built on Long Island.

"You bought a huge barn and had it hauled to your property... *miles away*. Then, when a building contractor told you it was impossible to connect the barn to your printing plant because it would cause the barn to *collapse*, you picked up a sledgehammer and personally knocked a hole between the two buildings.

"You bought the contents of a bankrupt coffee shop and had your *own* coffee shop built on your property. You converted that property to

Red Pen Corner with offices and workrooms. You hired an army of your own employees. Your own business *empire*! I'm running out of breath."

Bob was moved by his brother's praise. "Get your breath, brother," he said. "And thank you."

"I could keep talking," Richard continued. "About your goodness and generosity to your family—your parents, your relatives, your sister and me. Your generosity to the community—financing baseball teams, football teams, basketball teams. Your generosity to all kinds of charities. I'm running out of breath again."

Bob's voice was thick with grateful emotion. "Better save it for your own declaration," he told his brother.

Richard sighed heavily. "I'm almost sorry I mentioned that," he murmured.

"*Good*," Fanny said. "We've had enough."

"No, *not* enough, sister," Sven said seriously. "We've all had our cards laid out on the table."

"Not quite," Francis said, looking at Gladys.

"*Right*," she appeared to submit. "I'm an alcoholic, a bank robber and a Russian spy."

"I thought so," Sven reacted with pseudo-grimness. Almost everyone laughed.

"And, with that confession, I will now go home," Gladys said.

"*Not yet*," Richard told her.

"I thought you were sorry you mentioned your declaration," she said.

"I am, but I'm going to do it anyway," Richard replied.

"And I have something to do with it?" she asked.

He smiled. "Sort of," he said.

"I'll gird my loins," Gladys said. She grimaced. "I mean I'll get myself ready."

"Richard," Mary said.

He looked at her questioningly.

"I thank you for all the nice things you said about my husband," she told him.

"Yes. Bravo for those kind words," Sven said, clapping his hands. Everyone applauded. Bob smiled embarrassedly.

"Thank you all," he murmured.

"I meant every word," Richard said to Mary.

"I know you did. God bless you," Mary responded.

"Okay, okay," Sven said with make-believe resentment. "Enough of this *love-fest* stuff. Let's get back to the nitty-gritty."

Richard sighed audibly. "The nitty is pretty gritty, Uncle," he said.

"Do we have to?" Fanny asked her son.

"After everyone has had their say?" Richard confronted her.

"Not me," Tollef said.

"*Yes*," Sven declared. "*What about you*? Still an alcoholic? Still a Swedish spy?"

"Russian," Tollef said. "I don't like the Swedes."

"You heard it, folks," Sven announced. "Tollef Nelson has declared himself a Russian spy. Okay, now I'll confess. I'm a Czechoslovakian agent."

"You're a fool," Evelyn said.

"That too," he admitted.

"All right, what about that declaration?" Vivian demanded of her cousin.

"Yes. What about it?" he worried.

"Aren't you going to make it" Francis asked.

"I guess," Richard said, dubiously.

"*Why not*?" Francis went after him.

"To avoid more pain?" Richard suggested.

"Did *I* avoid pain?" Francis asked.

"Not much of it," Evelyn said, gently.

"None of us did," Bob said. He smiled. "Go for it, brother mine."

"*All right*," Richard agreed firmly. Then relapsed into uncertain silence.

"*Well*?" Vivian demanded.

Richard drew in a full breath before he began. "All right," he said. "The one thing this family never talks bout – that I've never heard anyway—is *sex*."

"*Oh*, ho," Bob's reaction was one of humorous apprehension.

"Well, *have* we? *Ever*?" Richard queried the table.

"Leave me out," Sven said. "I never discuss politics."

"It's not something people talk about, Richard," Evelyn said.

"No, it's not," Fanny concurred.

"Why?" Gladys asked, so softly as to be barely audible.

"Yes, *why*?" Richard had heard his sister and was echoing her. "Is it such a horrendous subject?"

"*It's something people do not talk about*," Fanny said.

"*You* people, you mean!" Richard contested. "You and Tante Evelyn! I don't know about the rest of us."

"You should spend an afternoon with *my* family," Mary said. "It would curl your hair."

"Now that we're into it," Bob contributed. "Never in my life have I run across a group of people so dedicated to sexual repression."

"Bravo," Tollef said. They all looked at him. Some in shock, (Evelyn and Fanny) some in delight, (Bob, Mary and Richard) some in pleased startlement, (Francis and Vivian) one in open-mouthed amazement, (Uncle Sven.)

"*Tollef*." It was all Evelyn could say.

"Well, why not?" he replied.

"Bravo, Pop," Francis said, grinning.

Evelyn looked at Tollef questioningly. "We'll talk about it later," she said.

"Yes, we will," he told her. "There are too many questions in this house."

Evelyn changed her expression to one of curiosity but said no more.

"So, what do you say now?" Richard asked his mother.

"I have nothing to say," she told him.

"All right," Richard said. "I'll be specific then. What would you say if I told you that, when I was a teenager, I fantasized about going to bed with my sister?"

His mother had nothing to say about that. She was thunderstruck.

"You too?" Bob said.

This doubly thunderstruck Fanny. It made Richard laugh. Gladys looked as stunned as her mother.

"Shocked, Gladys?" Richard asked.

She didn't answer for several moments. Then she said, "Not as much as you think."

"Which means?" Richard asked in surprise.

"Which means *I know*," she said.

"And were repelled?" Bob asked.

"Not much," she said. "Hell, let's be honest. *Not at all*."

"*Gladys*," her mother really looked shocked now.

"Oh, come on, Mom," Gladys said. "I was supposed to be repelled that two extremely handsome young males wanted to make love to me?"

"*Gladys*." It was all Fanny could say. Utterly stupefied now.

"And here I thought drinking was the main problem in the family," Sven said.

"Oh, now *you* come on, Uncle," Bob went after him. "Are you playing Holy of Holies now? You never had an incestuous impulse in your life?"

"*Well…*" Sven said. Reluctantly. Everyone but Evelyn and Fanny had a good laugh. "If truth-telling is really the order of the day…" he began to confess.

"Must we really?" Fanny pleaded.

"You have nothing to worry about, Fasa," Sven assured her, almost seriously. "You were entirely too angelic to make time with. Alicia was *too beautiful*. It made her snooty." He turned to Evelyn with an overdone expression of pseudo-desire.

"This is a nightmare," Evelyn responded in pseudo-disbelief.

"Kiss muh, muh fool," Sven said.

"I'll *kick* you, you fool," his sister said.

Tollef was laughing the hardest. "Oh, hush up," she told him. "It's not *that* hard to believe." Tollef shook his head, brushing tears from his eyes.

"Not at all," Sven said. "You were as cute as a button," he paused. "Still are," he added.

Evelyn was laughing now. "See me later," she said. Now Vivian laughed the hardest. "*Mom?*" Francis said, not sure how he felt.

"All right, back to sex," Vivian said.

"*Sister*," Evelyn said in shock. She didn't even notice her verbal mistake.

Richard got right for it. "You remember Mr. Estes, Mom?" he asked.

"Yes. I remember him," Fanny answered. "Why?"

"Do you *remember* him?" he emphasized.

Her voice grew tight. "*Yes. I remember* him. *Why?*"

"Do you remember that he was queer?" Richard asked.

Fanny looked confused. Bob started to say something but Mary stopped him.

"A *homosexual*, mom," Richard said. A moment of silence passed. He still wasn't sure his mother understood. "*He had sex with men*," he said, raising his voice.

Fanny was pained and irritated at the same time. "*I understand*," she said. "Why are you telling me?"

Richard drew in a labored breath. "*Because he had sex with me*," he told her.

The only ones who didn't look startled were Bob and Mary. "Yes," Mary said. "No surprise," Bob regarded his brother with sympathy.

"*Richard...*" Evelyn murmured.

"Did you *have* to tell us this?" Fanny asked her son.

"*Yes*! I *did*!" Richard answered angrily. "I *did*!"

"*Bully*," Francis said.

"*Damn right*," Vivian added, invoking a stricken look from her mother.

"*There she goes, Miss America*," Sven sang under his breath.

"You get the picture, Mom?" Richard demanded. "Mr. Estes took me to his apartment, gave me wine to drink—"

"You *drank?*" Fanny said, aghast.

"Yes! As if it matters, Mom!" Richard cried. "The Devil's Brew! I don't remember whether it had any effect on me. All I *do* remember— I was only *fifteen*, for Christ's sake!—Sorry, for goodness sake—all I remember is we took off all our clothes and lay on the floor – the carpeting; in the sixty-nine position."

"Pal, you don't have to go into detail," Bob cautioned his brother.

"Yes, I do," Richard told him. "It's time Mom was told everything." He turned to his mother. "The sixty-nine position means we were lying in reverse—his genitals in my face, mine in his. He put my penis—I trust you know what that is—it's called the same thing in Norway."

"Richard, please," his mother begged.

"Enough, nephew," Sven said. Serious now.

"*No*, Uncle. I want my mother to hear it all."

"Wasn't it enough that you craved to boff your sister? Now *this*?" Sven said.

"*Boff*, Uncle?" Richard asked, laughing. "Where did *that* come from?"

"Maybe Uncle Sven was more a man of the world than we give him credit for," Bob said.

"Guilty as charged," Sven replied. A few disconnected laughs.

"Back to my story," Richard said.

"Must we?" his mother asked.

"Yes, Mom. *We* must," he said. "Mr. Estes and I were naked, head to toe. He put my penis in his mouth and started to—"

He broke off as Fanny jolted to her feet, crying out. "I won't listen to this filth!"

"Sorry, Mom," Richard said. He didn't mean a word of it. "It's all untrue, of course. I made it up to shock you."

"Well, you succeeded!" his mother's voice cracked as she spoke.

"Jesus Christ, Mom!" Richard lamented furiously. "Don't you get *anything*? I didn't make it up! It *happened*!"

"Did you—?" Bob started hesitantly.

"Do the same to him?" Richard interrupted. "I tried for a few seconds, but it was too hot and I had to stop."

"So he didn't—?" Mary said, also hesitant.

"Come in my mouth? No," Richard's tone was close to brutal, directed at his mother.

"Well, that's something," Mary commented irrelevantly. It made Richard chuckle, not with amusement.

"Thanks for trying," Richard told her. He looked at his mother. "Well, Mom, nothing to say?"

"Don't overdo it, Dick," Bob told him.

Fanny was so choked up she could barely speak. "How often — ?" she began, unable to continue.

Richard remained furiously incredulous. "How *often?*" he said, laying it on cruelly. "Oh... at least five times a week for three years."

"*Dick,*" his brother cautioned.

"*Twice on Sunday,*" Richard went on regardless. "Once after church, once before dinner."

"*Come on,* Richard," his brother cautioned further.

"I don't believe you," Fanny said.

"Well, wonder of wonders," Richard said. "A glimmer of light. You're right, Mom. I was making it up. To be mean. I apologize. It happened *once.* Never again."

"*Thank God,*" Fanny said.

"*Ay — men,*" Vivian sarcasted.

"Mom, I still don't think you get the point," Richard said to her.

Fanny was sitting down again. "Which is — ?" she asked.

"Why did you let me go out with him at all? To Washington, D.C. for God's — for *goodness* — sake?"

"Is that where he abused you?" she asked.

"*Abused* me?" Richard went into fury again. "Jesus Christ, Mom! He wasn't the Marquis De Sade! He was James T. Estes. A pleasant, middle-aged man who taught High School music who just happened to be — " he bleated the word, "*Queer!*"

"That really is enough, Richard," Bob said.

Richard nodded. "You're right." But he turned to his mother. "I just want to make sure you understand. No, it wasn't in Washington where he 'abused' me. It was in his apartment in Brooklyn. I thought I told you."

She only shook her head. Richard cast his eyes skyward; wondering if she had gotten the point yet.

"Mom, you must have known—at least *suspected*—that Mr. Estes was *effeminate*. If you know what I mean."

"I *know*," Fanny sounded irritated now. She added, "I may not have completed my schooling but I'm not stupid."

"Bravo, Fanny," Evelyn said.

"Good, Mom," Gladys added.

"I never thought you were stupid, Mom," Richard told her, feeling a twinge of guilt. "You're a very intelligent woman. I can't believe he gave you no idea at all about the kind of man he was." He waited. "*Mom?*"

She answered defensively. "I thought he was lonely because he had no children," she said.

That was a new one on Richard. "You really thought that?"

"*Yes*, dear. I *did*," her voice was no longer that of the accused but that of a stern mother to her disobeying son.

"His personality didn't bother you at all?" he kept on.

"*No*, dear. It *didn't*," she said.

"What about you, Bob?" Richard asked his brother. "You must have met him."

"A few times," Bob said.

"And it didn't bother you that I was seeing him?" Richard asked further.

"As a matter of fact, it did," Bob told him.

"But you never said anything about it to Mom?" Richard guessed.

"No, as a matter of fact, I did," Bob told him.

"What did you say?" Richard asked.

"That I didn't think it was a good idea for you to see the man," Bob answered.

"What did you say to that?" Richard asked his mother.

"I said that Mr. Estes was the conductor of the Y-Boys Songsters," she told him.

"*And—?*" Richard pursued.

"And that you went to rehearsal twice a week," she said.

"*Rehearsal*, Mom," Bob contested. "I wasn't talking about rehearsal. All the boys were at rehearsal. I was talking about *personal contact*."

"Well, obviously I didn't understand that," his mother responded tensely.

"Well, I'm sure you understood that I was against Richard being taken to Washington."

"D.C.," Francis added.

"*Yes*," Bob said, wincing slightly at the pointless correction.

"Well, obviously I didn't know what you were talking about," Fanny said.

"Yes, *obviously*," Bob answered.

"No need for that, Robert," she said.

Bob sighed. Mary patted his hand.

"I apologize, Bob," Richard told him. "I didn't know you'd said anything."

"Well, we *did*, Richard," Gladys spoke. "Now that the subject's come up."

"You, too?" Richard was impressed.

"Yes. Me too," she said. "I thought Mom understood."

"Poor Mama didn't understand anything in those days," Fanny said. Her tone self-pitying.

"*In those days?*" Vivian said.

Fanny bristled. "*You have something to say, Vivian?*"

Vivian sighed, giving in. "No, sorry," she mumbled.

"So are we through?" Richard asked.

"Through?" Evelyn added to the question.

"Talking about sex," Richard said.

"I hope so," Fanny wished.

"Well, we're *not*, Mom," Richards told her. "At least, we shouldn't be."

"Good evening, Mr. and Mrs. America," Sven mimicked Walter Winchell.

"Under ordinary circumstances we *wouldn't* be talking about sex, Mom," Richard continued. "But these aren't ordinary circumstances."

"Apparently not," Fanny said.

"Well, they're not, Mom," Richard declared.

"He's right, Mom," Mary supported him.

"We've heard things today we've never heard before," Richard said to his mother. "*Valuable* things. *Necessary* things."

"*Bully*," Francis congratulated. "*Double* Bully." He exchanged a thumbs-up with his cousin.

"Well, I'll be going home now," Fanny said. "Gladys?"

Gladys hesitated for several moments before replying, "Not yet, Mom."

"You said Bernie has to go to work," Fanny pushed.

"*Not yet, Mom*," Gladys told her.

Fanny blew out weary breath. "Well, fine," she said. "I'll just sit here and pray to God I go deaf."

"*You don't really mean that, Mom*," Gladys told her sternly.

"*Everybody's* going after me today," Fanny said.

"No one's going after you, Mom," Bob tried to reassure her. "We're just trying to understand things."

"*Fine things*," she said.

"Oh, hush up, Mom," Gladys told her. "Just sit there and listen. Don't go deaf."

"Don't be mean to your mother, Gladys," Evelyn appealed.

Gladys didn't respond. Instead, she looked at Richard. "When you were telling your—*story*—was it necessary to be so... *graphic*?"

"No," he said. "It wasn't. *Yes, it was!*" he changed his mind. "I wanted what happened to take front and center in our play."

"Our *play*?" she questioned.

"Our theatre then," he said.

"Our *theatre*?" Vivian asked.

"*Okay!*" he said impatiently. "*The Nelson Family Room Theatre* then! I wanted to see that what was happening stayed alive!"

"We understand," Mary said.

"I'm twenty-eight years old!" he ranted on. "I've spent a lot of time with this family! Have I ever heard a word—a hint—a *breath*—anything at *all* about sex? You tell me."

"No," Bob said. "Not a word."

"That's right," his brother agreed. "Despite the fact that every one of us has a physical body, you'd never know it in this family."

"True," Bob said. "We all have souls presumably—but—"

"Not *presumably*," Fanny broke in.

"Except for me," Sven said. "I'm not so sure about me."

"Sven, shame on you," Evelyn told her brother.

"The point *is*," Bob went on. "We definitely have bodies. Francis has a body. He's an adult. He has physical needs. So what? Does that make him a criminal?"

He looked at Vivian. "Vivian is a grown woman," he continued. "She has physical needs."

"Sexual needs," Richard enlarged.

"Puh-*leeze*," Vivian objected. Not too strenuously.

Richard smiled. "I don't know about my sister," he said.

"*Richard*," Gladys warned him.

"Her condition gives an idea," Richard went on.

"*Enough*," Gladys said. But she was smiling too.

"I don't know about Mary," Richard said.

"This is terrible," Evelyn said.

"We'll get to you later," Sven promised.

"You better not," Evelyn said.

"Mary *does* have a body though," Richard said. "Not to mention five children, though."

"All found under cabbage leaves, no doubt," Sven said.

Vivian snorted. Mary and Bob laughed. "You both know what I'm talking about though," Richard said to them.

"Of course we do," Mary answered.

"Do we really have to talk like this?" Fanny asked.

"Like *what*, Mom?" Richard said. "*Honestly*? *Factually*?"

"*Offensively* would be a better word," she countered.

"It all depends," he said.

"On *what*?" she demanded.

"On who's offended," he told her. He drew in a deep breath. "Look, it really doesn't matter about the rest of us," he said. "All that matters is that we know we have bodies and those bodies have needs."

"And that we can *talk* about it," Francis added.

"*Exactly*," Richard nodded.

"But everybody *won't* talk about it," Vivian said.

"Maybe they will now," Bob suggested.

"I *doubt* it," she rebuffed.

"Well, keep hoping," Mary said.

"And leave the rest to history," Bob added.

"Profound," Sven said.

"And now I really have to go," Gladys told them. "Bernie *has* to go to work."

"No more sex talk?" Vivian asked.

"Vivian, in the name of God—" Evelyn started.

"*What does God have to do with it*?!" Vivian cut her off.

"Oh, sis," her mother said unhappily. "Yes, I know."

"God has to do with *everything*, Vivian," Fanny told her.

"Oh… *nuts*," Vivian reacted.

"Mom, are you ready?" Gladys asked her.

"*More than ready*," Fanny said, getting up.

Gladys stood. "Let's go, then," she said. After a moment, she looked at Richard. "And thank you for the things you said," she looked at her older brother. "Both of you," she said. "It was nice to hear."

"I'm relieved," Richard said. "I thought it was all my diseased fantasy."

"It wasn't diseased," she told him. "It was lovely."

"*Gladys*," Fanny appealed.

"I wouldn't have *done* it, Mom!" Gladys lashed at her.

"I'm disappointed," Richard said.

"*Shush*," Gladys told him. She turned back to her mother. "I would not have committed *incest*, mother!" she said. "It's just lovely—to *me*—to find out that my brother's thought of me in that way. What's so terrible about that?"

Fanny's reply sounded helpless. "I don't know, anymore, what's terrible and what isn't. I only know what I believe."

"Fasa," Sven said. "Would it help any if I told you that I really *did* have a yen for you?"

"*Oh, for God's sake*, Sven!" she cried. But she was laughing.

"His sake has been requested an awful lot today," he said. "He must be getting tired of it."

"Don't be profane, brother," Evelyn said.

"Well, I had a yen for Alicia, too," he told her. "Put me in jail."

"I'd love to," she told him.

"This day has become impossible," Fanny said, no longer laughing.

"Hear, hear," Evelyn cheered.

"No, not impossible at all," Sven disagreed. He was serious now. "A revelation. To how many of us, I don't know. Certainly to me."

"Me, too," Francis said.

"I give up," Fanny surrendered.

"Don't give up," Sven told her. "Take it all in. Chew on it. Spit out what you don't want. Or can't deal with. But *keep the rest.*"

"And *profit from it,*" Richard urged.

"*Ay-men,*" Vivian said. Now she was sincere.

"We'll try," Tollef said. Evelyn started to say something, then couldn't find the words.

"That's all we ask," Francis said. "Uncle Sven is right. This day *is* a revelation. Really."

"We'll be going now," Gladys said.

Richard grinned. "I'll walk you to your car."

Fanny headed toward the parlor to get her coat. Richard got up and helped Gladys with her chair. Tollef stood to say good-bye to everyone.

"Fanny, wait," Evelyn said. Rising, she followed her sister into the parlor. Sven got up as well as Francis and Vivian.

"Time for the family fuck-up to depart," he said. Francis and Vivian laughed. Bob and Mary got up. Bob smiling. "Uncle," he said. They shook hands.

"Nephew," Sven said. "It's been—what did you call it?—an *event.*"

"That's for sure, Uncle," Bob said. "It's been good seeing you again."

"Same here, Robert," Sven replied. He patted Bob on the arm.

Mary gave Sven a hug. "Good-bye, Uncle," she said. "Sorry I cussed at you."

"No problemo," he reassured her.

"You made me laugh," she told him.

"My role in life," he said.

He gave Vivian a hug. "Vivian, my dear." he told her. "You impressed me."

"Ditto, Uncle," she said.

"My cup runneth over," he responded. He kissed her on the cheek. "Carry on, niece," he said.

"I will," she promised.

"*Excellent*," Sven praised her. "You, too, Francis."

"Right on," Francis told him. Sven smiled.

Sven turned to Tollef now. "Tollef!" he said.

"Good to see you, Sven," Tollef replied.

"And good to see *you*, Tollef," Sven said. "Was it good for you to hear everyone speak as they did?"

"Quite interesting," Tollef admitted.

"And you'll keep it all in mind?" Sven probed.

"I will," Tollef said. "Count on it."

"Good, good," Sven repeated, pleased.

"Double good," Vivian said. She hugged her father and he embraced her back. "My dear," he murmured.

"Oh, *Pop*!" she said. It was the first time that afternoon she sounded happy. "*Thank* you!" She almost started to cry.

"I'll talk to your mother," Tollef assured her. He looked at Francis. "About you too, son."

"Thank you, Pop," he said. He hugged his father, then Sven. "Thank you too, Uncle," he said.

"You're welcome, nephew." Sven said. "I don't know what I did in particular—but if any of it was useful, I'm rewarded."

"You should be," Francis said. He turned to Gladys who was standing nearby with her younger brother. "*Cousin Gladys*," he said, beaming at her.

"*Cousin Francis*," she responded in kind. "God bless you."

"God bless you, too, Cousin Gladys," he said.

"*God bless us, everyone*," Richard piped up.

"What?" Vivian asked. She had stopped crying and was dabbing at her eyes with the handkerchief her uncle had handed her.

"Just being silly," Richard told her.

"*Oh*," her tone was flat. Silliness was not her cup of tea that day.

Gladys cheek kissed goodbye to all of them and turned toward the parlor, Richard with her.

"*Glad?*" he whispered.

"*Yes*," she whispered back, half smiling.

"Did you really know?" he asked.

"Well, I couldn't swear on a stack of Bibles, but I think so," she answered.

"Wouldn't you have worried about getting pregnant?" he asked.

"Oh, dear God," she said, laughing. "Mom would have had a seizure."

"Me, too," he admitted.

"Well, then it's just as well it never happened," she teased.

"God, *don't* say that," he said.

Gladys quieted him. Fanny and Evelyn were talking in the front hall, within hearing range. "Goodbye then," Richard whispered. He kissed her on the lips and she didn't pull away.

"What a day this has been," she said.

"*What a rare mood I'm in*," he said softly. Gladys laughed and patted him gently on the cheek.

All of them were in the parlor now. General goodbyes and cheek pecking took place. Coats and hats were donned.

"Thank you, Tante," Gladys said.

"If there was anything to thank me for," her aunt said.

"Lemon cake?" Gladys asked lightly.

"I knew there had to be something," Evelyn said, nodding.

"Well, goodbye to The Terrible Tantes," Sven said.

"*Oh, you,*" Fanny slapped him on the arm. No pain was intended or received.

"Just don't forget our Ha Ha Club. Friday night," Evelyn told him.

"Wouldn't miss it for the world," Sven said. "Well, maybe for the world." General chuckles.

"Goodbye Tante, Uncle Tollef," Bob said. "If anything untoward was said – "

"Too much was said," his mother interrupted.

"You still think that?" He sounded disappointed.

"No, she doesn't," Evelyn said. She cut off her sister's objection. "You *don't*, Fasa. You just told me so."

Fanny sighed. "Ah, well…"

Bob hugged her. "You're a clever girl, Fasa," he told her with a grin.

"So they say," she muttered. Bob and Mary laughed together.

"Pop said you'd talk," Vivian said to her mother.

"We will, dear. We will," Evelyn promised. Vivian didn't look totally convinced.

"There's a lot of talking to be done," Tollef said. Vivian smiled at him. Evelyn regarded him as though she hadn't seen him before.

"Yes," Sven said. "To begin with, why on Earth do we call our Friday night bridge game — The Ha-Ha-Club?"

Evelyn's smile was tired. "I don't know, Sven," she said. "There seems to be a lot of things I don't know."

"*Right*," Francis said, succumbing to bad taste. "*Hey*! *Viv*! You wanna go to bed with me?!"

"*Francis*," Evelyn pleaded weakly.

"Why the hell not?" Vivian responded to her brother. "Let's have a stiff drink first!"

"*Oh, my*," Evelyn said. She knew they were putting her on but it still dismayed her.

"Well, you wanted a happy home," Sven poked fun.

"Just shut up," she said, wearily. More laughter. Except from Evelyn and Fanny.

"*You're on the way, Mom*," Francis told her proudly.

"—to where I do not know," she completed a poem she partially remembered.

"Neither do I," Fanny said.

Gladys took her mother's arm. "Good night, all," she said as they went out.

"Good lord, is it night already?" Sven said. He looked toward the windows. "Not quite," he said. "It *is* raining though. Or is that sleet? Don't tell me it's sleet."

"It's sleet," Francis told him. He laughed. "I know, you told me not to tell you," Sven patted him on the back.

"*Au revoir, all*," Sven said. He hugged Evelyn "Especially you, Evelina," he patted her on the behind. "*Au revoir*, sis."

She pulled away. "You're awful," she said.

"And you're a cutie-pie," he told her.

"No, I'm not," her smile was pleased. "But thanks."

"Keep an eye on this cutie-pie," Sven said to Tollef.

"You're making me jealous," Tollef replied.

"No," Sven said. "You don't have a jealous bone in your body. For that matter, I don't think you have a *bone* in your body. You're too good-natured. You *bend* too easily."

Tollef wasn't sure why he was laughing. He'd mull over it later. Especially in light of the pleading look Vivian gave him.

Sven waived as he walked into the front hall. "*Au revoir*," he said. "*Auf Weidersein. Arriverderci. Toodle-oo*." He completed his farewell in Norwegian. "Don't take any spoiled Gjtost." (A sweet cheese resembling brown laundry soap.)

"What a terrible man," Evelyn said, smiling.

"I heard that," Sven said before he closed the front door. Laughter followed him.

Bob and Mary hugged Tante Evelyn and thanked her. They said good-bye to Uncle Tollef, who said, "Come again."

"*No, thank you*," Mary joshed. Tollef laughed. So did his son. Bob and Mary left. Everyone was gone but Richard and his aunt. After Francis and Vivian went upstairs, Tollef returned to the family room to help clean up. Before he left, Evelyn kissed him on the cheek and called him "Nissa-gullah," a Norwegian term of endearment. It made Tollef smile.

Evelyn looked at her nephew. "How will you get to your brother's house?" she asked.

"Oh, he'll wait for me. I'll only be a moment."

She smiled. "Well, your declaration was sure a doozy."

"Not too much of a doozy I hope," he said.

"You hope in vain," she responded, half in humor.

"Sorry, Tante," he said. "I want to tell you I know you had to face some big emotional blows this afternoon."

"So did your mama," she reminded him.

"I know, but you handle yours better," he said. "At least you seemed to."

Mama will handle hers too," she told him. She gave him a hug and kissed him on the cheek.

"Would you do something for me, Tante?" he asked.

"Do I dare say yes?" she asked back.

Richard smiled, then said, "Would you tell Fran that I'd really like him to come to California after he gets that surgery?"

"Surgery," she murmured.

"You know he has to have it, Tante. I know he's a Christian Scientist; in this case, that isn't enough. *He needs surgery.*"

She sighed heavily. "*Does* he?" she said.

He only looked at her. She sighed again. "I know," she said.

She walked with him toward the front hall. "Y'know," he said. "Maybe we all learned something today."

"Well, we learned that my brother Sven has a big mouth," she said.

He grinned. "But a funny one," he altered. The grin faded. "You *saw* it happen, Tante," he said seriously.

Outside, Bob honked his car horn. "There, I told you he'd wait," Richard said. Then, "It was all inside us, Tante. We just didn't expect it to all come out in one afternoon," he grunted with dark amusement. "And after a funeral at that."

"Bertolf didn't miss a thing," she said. They exchanged a smile.

He gave her another hug and cheek kiss.

"Good-bye, Tante," he said. He paused. "I love you," he added.

That really got to her. She hugged him back so vigorously that he grunted again, this time with an amused gasp.

"I love you too, darling," she told him. "I love everyone in the family," she made a tiny sound of amusement. "Even those who aren't so crazy about me."

"We're all crazy about you, Tante," he said. "You're a Norsky cutie-pie." He kissed her on the cheek again. "Good-bye."

After he'd gone, Evelyn stood motionless for a while, then walked to the family room and began helping her husband clean up. While she was doing it, she gave Tollef a hug and kiss.

Then she began singing, "Sweetheart, Sweetheart, Sweetheart. Will you love me ever?"

Outside, the sleet turned gradually to gentle rain.

~~~~~

I have, in this account, referred to my father without ever bringing him to life. The following was written years ago.

~~~~~

I almost cried out in horror when I saw my father lying in his coffin like some hideous painted doll. The face I knew was pasty and lifeless. I could hardly bear to look at him. When my aunt asked me if I wasn't going to kiss him goodbye I was struck with terror and couldn't move. I could never have put my lips on that cold skin.

I hated the funeral. It was dismal and morbid. Some thin old man from our church performed a sort of ritual over him. I sat there and felt the hair rising on my scalp. I thought my father was listening. I thought any moment he would sit up and tell us all to go home and leave him in peace.

I was disgusted with the meaningless chatter that relatives use at funerals when they haven't seen each other for years. Asinine prattle about how so and so has grown and how terrible a blow this was to them and how natural he looks. God! Always how natural he looks. Whispers of his last painful moments, his contorted face and sweat of agony all resolved now into gentle and everlasting lines. I hated all that.

When it was all over we went back into the sunlight. To me it was like coming back from the dead. Back to the harping world, the clang of trolley cars, the sound of heels on the sidewalk, the breaths of a living comet. I left my father behind. Soon he would be in darkness and they would throw dirt over his face.

My mother went to the burial. I went home with my aunt and uncle. When we reached their car I put a handkerchief on the seat for my aunt. *He* was always a gentleman. That's what she said. In tones indicating that he was nothing else. Maybe she was right. I'll never know.

When we got to their apartment, we went up and talked a while. She had just lost her son. I guess that was why she felt morbid about it. Death was almost an acquaintance.

Then I went down to the bakery to buy some cake. I knew I wouldn't eat any. I couldn't eat for a long time after seeing him lying there with his thin hands on his chest and that ugly brown suit they had placed on him. It was false. Everything was false. If I could only have believed in immortality.

While I walked to the store I began to think of him. There wasn't much to think about.

When I was very small he was only another face, a voice among voices. When I was a little boy I hardly ever saw him. He was working and I had to go to bed before he came home. Once in a while he came in and talked to me. I never understood him. I was sleepy and his voice was a far off drone and I fell on the pillow. He would kiss me on the forehead and go out, closing the door silently behind him. Now he was dead and I was only fifteen. What could I remember? The bad things? Yes, I could remember the bad things.

I remembered his drinking. Remembered how he stayed away from home for long periods of time and then returned, contrite, for many weeks. Before I got to know him at all he was living by himself and I was with my mother and sister.

I remember the day I went to camp. He came by the house and I had both my mother and father to take to the bus with me.

I sat inside and talked with them. I couldn't tell whether they were strangers to each other. I was going to camp and I only knew I'd cry before they were even out of sight.

I kissed my mother and shook hands with him and waved until the bus turned the corner. Then I cried.

Later they showed us movies of the busses going to camp. I saw my father standing there with his arm around my mother, waving to me. Why wasn't it always like that? Why wasn't he always there to wave to me and walk with me and tell me things only a father can tell a boy? What good is it to go to a ball game or a movie or bowling once in a while? Was I supposed to glory in a few moments of acting as if nothing were wrong? I wanted more than that but I never had it.

And now he was dead. I was fifteen and he was dead. Moving through the streets in his coffin to his last port.

And I remember the night he tried to beat me. I was all alone in the house. It was at a time when I missed my mother so much when I was alone that I sat and shivered until I heard her key in the door. I could never sleep. There were wild plans of getting up and walking down to the trolley station in my pajamas and waiting for her; of going down to church or wherever she was and standing there until she came out.

That was why I was glad when my father came in that night. He was drunk. I was very disrespectful. I made no secret of my scorn. He ate in silence and whenever he said anything I answered him in an insolent way.

Finally he got angry and chased me into my room and tried to beat me. I struggled and struck him on the face and cried out in tear-ridden anger.

Then I was sitting on his lap and he was talking to me gently. He tried to tell me that he loved me but that I should treat him with respect. I asked him to stop drinking but he brushed it aside and told me not to worry about that. I cried a little more and then he went back to his supper and I did my homework, choking every once in a while with a sob.

I remembered the Christmas Eve he came home drunk. I saw the look on everybody's face when he came in. They didn't know what to do so they joked about it. I never liked that. Trying to laugh at little incongruities in his thick speech. Trying to look amused while he fumbled terribly after insisting on carving the roast. Smiling at each other while he struggled to open his gifts and told us over and over again how sorry he was he didn't have enough money to give us presents. It wasn't funny. Not to be patronizing to your own father. It was ugly and tragic.

That night when everybody was asleep and he was snoring on his bed, I cried and buried my face in the pillow so no one could hear me.

In the morning when everybody was still asleep he got up and sat in the kitchen drinking coffee. When I came in he told me that a neighborhood theatre was putting on a morning show. He put some money in my hand and said I could make it if I hurried.

I didn't go. I told him I wanted to look at my presents. He told me to keep the money anyway "for a rainy day" and then went back to his proud silence.

If I had only gone. If I had only exulted over and over again what a wonderful show it was and how much I wanted to see it. If I had only grabbed my hat and coat and run out in glee so that I wouldn't miss a moment of it.

I didn't do that. I stayed home to look at my presents and his Christmas was lost.

And now I was fifteen and he was dead and there were no more chances. No more fears that he would come in and ruin our meals or our evenings. No more talks about him living alone and working at odd times. No more little amounts of money coming to my mother once in a while. It was all over.

Near the end of his life I went to visit him occasionally in his room. I try to remember what we ever talked about. I don't think we ever became more intimate than discussing my report card. He always signed that until he died. With his florid and wonderful signature that looked so important. I had the best signature in the class on my report card. Was that what he was my father for?

Then we'd walk down the street and I'd sit and drink lemonade and eat pretzels while he drank. I tried to look interested but soon I'd get down from the stool and mention that he'd promised to take me to the movies. And he'd give me the money and tell me he couldn't go and I'd better go myself. I had to walk away from him. Wondering what it would be like to walk in the park with him. Didn't he ever long for my company the way I longed for his? Didn't he want to go to the zoo or to the beach and romp? Why did he stay away from me?

Before he died he started to write a story of his life. If he had only finished it. I might know all the things I want to know. Was the chore too dull and tiring after living on the sea for years? Was the restraint of marriage too much after a lifetime of adventure?

In the beginning of his story he wrote that when he was a little boy of about seven years he climbed the mast of a schooner. He went all the way to the top and looked around and saw his home town far beneath on shore like a doll's city.

He said he felt like he was sitting near God, looking down at the world and wondering what could be done about it. There was no dizziness, no fright. He was high, high, almost up in the clouds, moving with the wind, looking down at a world that wasn't real at all but only a toy.

~~~~~

Vivian never married. Obese and embittered, she died in her seventies. Francis never had the operation. He drank himself to death in his fifties. Uncle Sven died of a heart attack in his seventies. Bob died of colon cancer at the age of sixty-five. Mary died several years later. Gladys died at the age of ninety-two. Living with Gladys, Fanny died at the age of ninety-two. Tante Evelyn died of a heart attack in her sixties. Uncle Tollef died in his sleep at the age of ninety-six. Richard wrote this book when he was eighty-four.

GENERATION

by

Richard Matheson

NEW PAGE

1. Parents and ~~children~~ ~~offspring~~ children.

2. Bringing ~~into~~ ~~awareness~~

NEW PAGE

TO MY FIRST FAMILY

NEW PAGE

OVERTURE

NEW PAGE
ACT ONE (P. 1)

The strangeness about this story that it

never happened. It could have happened. It might have

happened. For that matter, it should have happened. If there was

honesty and justice it certainly should have taken place

as I described it. Or close to it.

That's the thing you see. Many fiction writers have described

incidents from their past, containing actual dialogue and/or

declarations. That's where this account differs. The people described

were real. What isn't real is what they say. That isn't

exactly true. What they say, they might have said on a

similar occasion. That occasion never occurred. Accordingly,

all the revelations remained unspoken. Do I make myself

clear? The account never took place. Maybe fragments

of what is said were spoken here or elsewhere, other times,

not though. The point is that all those times really taken place

as I described them. To repeat: they should have

⚹   ⚹   ⚹

My family is pure Norwegian, what I mean ~~by~~

that is that all ~~the~~ family members, alive or not,

immigrated ~~from~~ Norway or ~~were~~ born of Norwegian ~~speaking~~ ~~parents~~ ~~descent~~

Later generations ~~lived~~ (and are) ~~not~~ ~~of course~~, not ~~pure~~ ~~pure~~ ~~totally~~

Norwegian ~~of course~~, I hope my will understand ~~his/custom~~ ~~my story~~ and not ~~tax~~

issue ~~want~~. [The ~~people~~ describes in my story are ∧ all pure ~~that~~ Norwegian

You will meet them one by one, my mother, brother

sister, ~~their~~ ~~family~~ Uncles, aunt and cousins. Pure Norwegian

every one of ~~them~~. Speaking words I never ~~heard~~ ~~them~~ heard them

speak but wish I had

      You have noticed, I'm sure, that I ~~have~~ not have

mentions my father. ~~He~~ was pure Norwegian too, but didn't

take ~~take~~ ~~part~~ ~~loose~~ part in ~~that~~ afternoon. He had been dead for ~~seven~~ ten years.

      It is funeral ~~was~~ is imagine, ~~by~~ ~~me~~, as having

taken place ~~in~~ in the early ~~afternoon~~ afternoon of my ~~story~~ account. His

~~death~~ date-altered ~~death~~ ~~was~~ demise is the genesis of the

gathering

*   *   *   *

The locale for my make-believe ~~story~~ account is ~~actual~~ real

enough. At least it was ~~on~~ ~~that~~ imagined afternoon in 1956.

Not that 1956 ~~was~~ is imaginary. It was what I say happened in 1956 that

didn't happen. Confusing enough? How else can I express it? It all

didn't happen ~~in~~ in a real house in a real year (to real people) Enough said

On with the story. I mean the ~~story~~ account.

The house of ~~its~~ the Lion~~Lawrence~~ Lawrence was on Bedford Avenue

in Flatbush. It was one of two houses wedged between a ~~business~~ brick office

~~brick~~ building and a Jewish temple. I have memories of the ~~rabbi~~ Rabbi

singing, the side door of the temple opened) On the ~~over~~ other side, the

~~business~~ office building had a ~~candy~~ Candy store in ~~its~~ corner. I remember my buying

ice cream cones there. They were called, to my ~~recollection~~ recollection, ~~Goss~~ GOBS.

My uncle Toller and ~~how~~ my aunt ~~Everette~~ Evelyn did

janitorial ~~help~~ cleaning in that building - one of the businesses must have been

a travel agency or something like it because they gave my ~~uncle~~ Uncle gazebo which

he rebuilt on his ~~back~~ yard. I ~~recall~~ recall many a ~~Sunday~~ Summer evening meal

enjoying in that ~~picture~~ open gazebo.

I also recall the ~~poses~~ police raiding one of the ~~of his~~

full of slot machines and breaking them up with sledge hammers.

My uncle took one of the ~~slot machines~~ home and repaired it. We

played with it often.

The house was two stories tall with three bedrooms

on the second floor, one bathroom. My cousin Francis

read one of one ~~bedroom~~ bedroom, about the size of a large closet.

We spent many an hour having fun in that diminutive room.

His sister Vivian had one of the other two bedrooms.

Uncle ~~Toilet~~ and ~~aunt~~ Evelyn had the third.

There was also an attic. In it, we called him

Francis ~~from~~ constructed cabin a ~~cars~~ airplane against a

wall. I was impressed. It complement, with two seats, full dashboard taken from an old car

a steering wheel and a small glass windshield. I was not permitted to

take the second seat. I was not that very companionable of that age, Francis

kept me in the ~~entry~~ by providing me with a single passenger boat which je

on the opposite side of the attic. It had no motor with

crawl-in cabin with a ~~miniture~~ minisule stove made of ply wood ~~with~~

and ~~five~~ two hooks for ~~a~~ heat control. I ~~wasn't~~ went crazy about it but

had no ~~place~~ other choice. I played my love character in ~~silen~~ wordless

silence.

* * *

It was one of ~~many~~ make-believe ~~melodramas~~ melodramas we ~~constructed~~ absorbed

~~ourselves in~~ There was also ~~story~~ complex plot populated by imaginary ~~characters~~ heroes

who flew model airplanes. Franny's ~~plane~~ was to be taken from,

I believe, Bill Barnes Air ~~Trails~~ a magazine called Trails. His plane was ~~the~~ as, I believe, called

the Snorter. Maybe not. ~~I can't~~ remember for sure ~~was the~~ * (INSERT)

name of ~~the~~ imagined hero. It was Kent Grayson. He always ~~won the~~ won the conte

, we had ~~aerial~~ resumes of our "teams", complete with faces

~~scissored~~ ~~by~~ from ~~the~~ Sears ~~Roebuck~~ a Roebuck catalog. ~~The~~ There was a head mechanic

called "Wing", which team he was on I ~~don't recall.~~ don't recall.

~~I remember~~ do recall that Franny's ~~copilot who~~ co-pilot, in attic plane after plane was.

~~was~~ George ~~Mulroy/Mulroy~~ a neighbor Mulroy George he was a pleasant, ~~cooperative~~ cooperative

game player/~~onlike me~~ ~~who~~ ~~was invariably/invariably~~ invariably

temperate. He never ~~complained~~ complained as I did.

(INSERT)

One more vivid memory. Francis owned

a beautiful Pistol which he utilized in many

of our imaginary dramas. One afternoon

George and I showed up at Francis' house

anticipating more entertaining dramatics. Instead,

we found a note left to us by our leader.

We were to cook in the area built above the

gazebo. There, to our shock, we found the beautiful

pistol in fragments. A grim note from Francis

he was now to play games. Accordingly, he was

destroying the Pistol. George and I were stricken

by the enormity of it. Game

Playing was over. George and I attempted to reinstate

it but, but that Francis was now use.

BACK
TO p 6

Franny was the absolute game-player in charge.

He was several years older than us. But it was more than

that. He was a leader. How this all played itself

big part of the tale unreal not never happening on everyone.

It didn't take place but should have. America.

———————— (INSERT) ———— * ———— * ———— *

The main locale for this never-happened happening

was the Ground floor of the Bedford Avenue house. Not exactly

the game room either. There was a front hall, a step-down

kitchen and a backyard where the gazebo had been re-built.

the account peripherally
the story, except peripherally did not occur in these parts

of the house's Ground floor.

Most of the story which never

took place took place in the family room of the

house. In September of 1956. Not that I ever heard it

referred to as the Family Room in those days

That's what that room was though. It was a room in

which/all family activities ~~activities~~ took place. ~~As you will see~~

The room adjoined the parlor which was ~~always~~ always

gloomily illuminated, even on a sunny ~~day~~ ~~day~~ because

of the ~~front~~ porch ~~roof~~ roof.

On the ~~other~~ side of what is call the Family Room ~~Room~~

was ~~the~~ a step ~~down~~ down doorway to the ~~kitchen~~ Kitchen. there was a door to

an oversize ~~large~~ closet on the ~~back~~ Back wall. ~~near~~ placed ~~the~~ ~~that~~ ~~door was an~~ enormous

~~round~~ ~~table~~ It had round ~~table~~ ~~table~~ with ten chairs around it, eight of them matching

the table, two ~~commandeered~~ commandeered from the Kitchen — on that particular ~~day~~ I suppose

day (that ~~it~~ ~~that~~ day which never took place ~~but should have~~) the ~~table was covered with platters of food~~.

Across the room from the table was an aged recliner

chair, its upholstery faded brown leather, a control button on top of

its right wooden arm. A floor lamp ~~stood~~ stood beside ~~the~~ the chair,

a sun-bleached shade on it.

The walls of the room ~~were~~ ~~lined~~ were lined with a ~~for several~~ number

of three of, time-worn, ~~glass~~ ~~fronted cabinets~~ glass-fronted cabinets in which "good"

dishes were displayed.

Almost covering the huge, round table was a flowered table cloth on which were arranged various the serving dishes platters. Some pseudo-crystal, some ordinary china, on the dishes were was a selection of edibles — Jewish Rye bread, and seeded dinner rolls, crackers and cheese slices spread, ham and salami (Cincinnati), sliced turkey, roast beef, mayonnaise, coffee cakes and vanilla cookies — Post funeral goodies,

The light in the room was dead in, were the afternoon outside overcast, a slight wind blowing

NEW PAGE ACT ONE

Evelyn Nelson came in from the kitchen, a large cake platter in her hands. She was fifty-nine years old, plump and grey-haired, pleasant, but not pretty face. She was wearing an unfashionable, flower-print dress and apron. She placed the cake platter down on the table and fussed with the table edibles, getting them arranged "just right." As she fussed she begins to sing "Sweetheart" from the Nelson Eddy-Jeanette MacDonald movie, her voice on key but ordinary & she is new or the

She was nearing the end of the story when

her daughter Vivian came in from the kitchen carrying

a small dish on which a ~~~~ quarter pound of ~~butter~~ butter

~~sat~~. Vivian was twenty-seven, not ~~~~ unpretty but overweight

with grey streaked brunette hair. She wore a long ~~~~

unattractive print dress and a long-sleeve ~~~~ gray sweater

Her comment was dry, "Bravo, Jeanette." she ~~said~~ said

"Silly," her mother muttered ~~~~ not amused "Is that

~~butter~~ on the crystal dish?"

"You mean the ~~plastic~~ fake crystal dish?" Vivian said

Her mother ~~~~ straightly ~~~~ slightly colored

"No Vivian's crystal" she said

Vivian ~~~~ slapped the dish onto the table.

"Imitation crystal, you mean." said ~~~~ she ~~~~ her

lips tightening as she turned back to the kitchen.

She almost collided with her brother as he

left the kitchen carrying a large electric coffee urn. Francis

~~Frank, as that now chosen to tell~~ was twenty-two years old,
five foot ~~ten~~ eight inches tall, slender and brunette. ~~He had~~ He had had
grown a mustache to hide, as ~~well~~ much as possible, a cleft palate.

His mother asked ~~him~~, "Is there enough coffee
left, do you think?"

"I don't know, Mom," ~~Grace~~ Francis ~~told~~ answered, moving toward the telephone. "Maybe
if ~~only~~ Uncle Sven and Uncle Bob are the only ones who drink it.

"You don't think Gladys, or Aunt Mary will?" his mother asked. ~~Evelyn asked~~
[with a deep sigh] ~~Francis~~ ~~turning~~ set the urn down on the ~~table~~. ~~I don't know~~
~~about~~ "Heavy," he said. He drew [a deep] ~~my~~ breath. "I don't know ~~about~~
Aunt Mary," he said, "Gladys usually drinks Postum like ~~Mom~~ her Mom"

An obese beagle came ~~strolling~~ waddling in from the parlor
Evelyn winced ~~grimaced~~. "Oh, dear," she said. She called out, "Sister! ~~That~~"

"Now what?" Vivian responded ~~sharply~~.

"Take Boots back to your room," Evelyn told her

"She was in my room!" Vivian called ~~back~~ back irritably

"Well, she's not there now!" Evelyn said. She leaned over the.

beagle to pat her head. "Sweetheart, you're not supposed to be in here," she said gently. Boots shook her ~~tail~~ wagged tail, quivering with pleasure.

"Boots, you nasty creature," Vivian said ~~softly as~~ she came in carrying a bowl of ~~fruit~~ apples, green grapes and bananas.

Evelyn made a pained sound. "She's not nasty," she said. "She just wanted to ~~join~~ (share in) the party."

"The party," Vivian ~~picking up~~

"You know what I mean," said her mother.

Vivian grabbed Boots ~~by her~~ by the collar and started ~~pulling her~~ dragging her across the ~~linoleum floor~~ "C'mon ~~the party~~ "C'mon Sweetheart," she muttered ~~softly~~.

"Don't hurt her," Francis ~~pleaded~~ told her.

"I'm not hurting her," Vivian ~~spit~~ ~~snarled~~ snapped back.

~~For the first time~~

"Turn on the light, Sam," Evelyn ~~broke in~~ told him, "It's getting ~~dark in~~ dark in here."